SLIPPING

SLIPPING

Cathleen Davitt Bell

BLOOMSBURY
CHILDREN'S
BOOKS

Published by Bloomsbury U.S.A. Children's Books
175 Fifth Avenue, New York, New York 10010
Distributed to the trade by Macmillan

Library of Congress Cataloging-in-Publication Data
available upon request
ISBN-13: 978-1-59990-258-6 • ISBN-10: 1-59990-258-3

First U.S. Edition 2008
Typeset by Westchester Book Composition
Printed in the U.S.A. by Quebecor World Fairfield
1 3 5 7 9 10 8 6 4 2

All papers used by Bloomsbury U.S.A. are natural, recyclable products
made from wood grown in well-managed forests. The manufacturing processes
conform to the environmental regulations of the country of origin.

For short young men past and future:
Michael, Rick, and Max

SLIPPING

Chapter 1

Let me start by saying that my grandpa had always been different. He didn't do the things other kids' grandfathers do. He didn't celebrate Thanksgiving or Hanukkah. He didn't decorate his living room with my sister's and my school pictures. He didn't send cards on my birthday. Once, I asked him why other grandparents did all these things, and Grandpa said he didn't believe in commercial excess.

I was only six then—I'm thirteen now—but I already knew "commercial excess" meant presents. We were sitting at the table in the one-room cabin next to a freezing lake where he lived all by himself in Vermont. He was peeling potatoes with a knife, because he didn't believe in vegetable peelers, and I was watching him because there was nothing better to do. "But I believe," I said.

Grandpa laughed, put down the knife, and clapped his hands. His hair was so short you could see through to the red of his scalp. "Who am I," he said, "Tinkerbell?"

Not that he believed in Tinkerbell. Or white bread. Or fresh milk—he drank powdered. He didn't believe in having a TV. When we visited the cabin, he and my dad listened to baseball games on the radio at night, and Mom, Julia, and I went straight to bed because we were so bored. During the day, after my lips turned blue from five minutes of swimming in Grandpa's lake, the most exciting thing to do was watch Grandpa chop wood with an ax. He would raise the ax high and yell, "Michael, stand back!" even when I was really, really far away. He taught me to play checkers—that was pretty cool—but he never let me win, even when I was, like, seven. And after I was seven, we didn't see Grandpa anymore.

My dad never said why we stopped going to visit. Dad isn't the kind of person who explains much. First of all, he works all the time, so I hardly ever see him. Second of all, he tends to turn questions around on you. Like, if I asked him, "How come we don't get to go see Grandpa anymore?" he'd probably just end up saying something like, "Do you know that 'get' is one of the most overused words in the English language?"

When I asked Mom why Grandpa stopped coming to see us, she sighed and said, "Oh, Grandpa," as if I'd asked a question that was far too complicated for her to explain. I asked her again, another time, and she said Grandpa didn't believe in New York. She said that he didn't call because he didn't believe in having a phone. I wondered if we had become one more thing not to believe in. I wondered if I believed in him either.

Then he died.

· · ·

It happened last month, February. I was taking a break from an earth science project, driving a Koenigsegg CC through the arches of the Musée d'Orsay—that's a building in my *Midtown Madness* Xbox game. I'm pretty sure it's in Paris. My video game privileges had been taken away after I got a C on my last earth science project, but my mom was too busy to notice. It was the week before one of Julia's ballet concerts, and when these are going on, my mom gets really distracted, and eventually disappears into a backstage haze of stapled costumes and helping the little kids put on eye shadow. Julia dances through the foyer, saying things like, "I am far too nervous to eat," which makes my mom too nervous to eat because it's her greatest fear in life that Julia will become anorexic. I try to explain to my mom that someone who always takes the last piece of pepperoni pizza probably doesn't have an eating disorder, but Mom worries anyway.

My dad came home from work late, as usual. He stood in the doorway to the dining room, which in our apartment is not where we eat together sitting around a table—the table is shoved against one wall, and an old beat-up couch and the TV live in the other corner. We eat in front of the TV. One of my mom's favorite jokes is to call our stack of take-out menus her cookbook.

Dad sort of slumped against the door frame and looked over at my mom. Everything about my dad is skinny, and everything about him shines, from his shoes, which he gets polished once a week in a little store in the basement of his office building, to his hair, which lies perfectly straight and flat, every single glistening black strand. He hates anything messy, which means he hates my room, and especially hates my hair.

3

He's a litigator—that's the kind of lawyer who argues with people all day. He works for himself, and Mom says he drives himself harder than any boss would, and that's why he's never home for dinner, and has to cancel vacations at the last minute. He's afraid that one day there'll be a big stock market crash and all the companies he protects when they get sued will go out of business and stop hiring him, and we'll have to sell our apartment, and Julia and I will have to stop going to private school. Dad is big into reminding us that private school is very, very expensive, and my mom is big into reminding Dad that we can totally, totally afford it.

He's always saying to me, "You have to pay attention. To things in the world. Something besides video games."

I'm not like my dad. He was a straight-A student who played three varsity sports and was president of the model UN. I'm the shortest kid in the eighth grade, including the girls. I'm bad at sports—everyone at Selden, my school, has to play, but when I hold a basketball up over my head to make a shot, I can feel it wobbling, while Mr. Ball, my coach, yells, "Pass it off. Pass it off." When Mr. Ball's picking the next sub during games, he looks right over my head.

My dad hates Mr. Ball. He'll say things like, "Don Ball's biggest fault as a coach is a lack of imagination. He'll never coach varsity." Of course, Don Ball's biggest fault as a coach is the fact that his last name is Ball, but whatever. I guess I should feel good that it makes my dad angry that Coach Ball doesn't play me. But it doesn't exactly feel like my dad's on my side. When he

4

comes to my games—which is, like, once a year—he always comes up behind me and covers my eyes. "What's the score, Michael?" he'll say. I never know.

I guess I take after my mom. She's really short like me, and she's always losing her house keys, and she never does the dishes until it's time to actually use the plates that are in the sink. One time I heard another mom ask mine how she managed with my dad working such long hours. My mom shrugged and said, "If I saw him more, maybe we'd find out we have nothing in common." My mom's like that—she talks about divorce, something my dad would never joke about. Or if he did, he'd say, "God forbid," even though he doesn't believe in God.

Now, while my dad was slumped in the doorway, Mom was talking on the phone and collating programs for Julia's ballet performance. She lifted her eyebrows to him, her sign that she was talking to a client. My mom is a freelance publicist specializing in consumer products, which she's always making us try, from the organic cinnamon-flavored toothpaste that actually tastes like sand to the body gel for girls that she tried to convince me could cross over.

My mom always laughs and gossips with clients like they're her friends, but never tells them to hold on, or asks if she can call them back. "Of course," she said now. "Naturally. Exactly." There are about five hundred ways to say "You're right," and my mom knows them all. She mouthed "Sorry" to my dad, then looked back down at the programs in a pile on her left, counting.

Instead of going into the kitchen to make himself a protein

shake, which is what he usually has for dinner, Dad kept watching her from the dining room doorway. My dad is someone who is never late, who is never wrong, who is never sad. But just then, he looked like he was maybe all three. He took a big breath in through his nose, and at the same time opened his eyes wide and lifted his eyebrows as far as they could go. Without waiting for my mom to hang up, he said, "My father died yesterday. It was a heart attack."

"Let me call you back," Mom said into the phone.

She stood still for a minute, staring. It was just a second that she paused before crossing the room to Dad. She put her arms around him even though he kept his at his sides. I wish I could say I felt sad hearing the news about Grandpa. But mostly I think I was curious, kind of waiting to see if I *would* feel sad. I had never known anyone who was dead before except my dad's mom, and she died before I was born, so that doesn't really count. Having Grandpa be dead was kind of like finding out he was famous.

The whole time Mom was hugging Dad, he never hugged her back. Mom's always making him kiss her hello or hold her hand in public. What's amazing to me is that not only will Dad kiss Mom back, he'll usually say something like, "Thanks for that," or laugh, like he's remembering a joke. Now, though, he didn't move, and when she finally let go, he said, "I have to review some files. I'll be in the kitchen," and left the room. He wasn't crying or anything.

My mom looked like she was the one who was going to cry, but instead, she pushed her hair up off her forehead and took a deep breath. She talks about how she should dye her hair back to brown, but then she just keeps letting it go grayer and grayer, and cuts it shorter and shorter. She's so short, and with her short gray hair, she kind of looks like a boy.

Watching my mom try not to cry, I lost control of the Koenigsegg. It spun out in the Place de la Concorde and crashed into the Seine River. Mom winced at the noise. "You," she said, "should be in bed. Turn that garbage off."

"First of all," I said, "video games are not garbage. This is teaching me about France. And second, if I go to bed, does that mean I don't have to finish earth science?"

"Yes. Whatever. No," Mom said.

"Which is it?"

"Bed!"

I climbed under my covers with my Game Boy, but before I turned it on, I heard Julia making goo-goo noises with our cat, Speckles. Julia's almost old enough to be getting a driver's license—that's seventeen in New York State—but most of the time she acts like she's nine.

"Julia," I called out, when I heard the water running in the bathroom that connects our two rooms.

"What?"

"Come here."

"Why?" She popped her head around the door. Julia has brown hair that's always brushed and shiny, and her nose is as straight as her perfect grades, perfect pink sweaters, perfect brown suede boots. Right now, the skin around her eyes was red from scrubbing. She's terrified of zits, even though she doesn't have any. Last year, she made Mom take her to the dermatologist to get a special anti-zit cream, and he said, "You have nothing to put it on." My dad loves to tell that story.

"Did you know Grandpa is dead?" I said. I expected she would. Mom and Dad treat her like a grown-up. They gave her her own American Express card. Next year, she'll be applying to college.

"Grandpa Kimmel?" she said. I don't know who else she could have thought I was talking about. We call our other grandfather Grands. Grands and Gaggy live on the sort-of farm where my mom grew up in Connecticut. They treat me like I'm five years old, it takes them about two hours to make pancakes, and they say things like "Okey-dokey" and "Jiminy Crickets." Last Christmas, after we visited them, Mom turned around in the driver's seat—Dad had gone back early, on the train—and said, "See, kids? I grew up in paradise and I chose to live in a place where you pay with your blood and sweat for a three-bedroom apartment. Who knows how you'll rebel."

"Yes, Grandpa Kimmel," I said to Julia now. There was something cool-feeling about finally knowing something before she did. "Dad just told Mom."

"Wow," Julia said. She pointed her toe, sliding her left leg out and tracing semicircles on the floor.

"Do you feel sad?" I asked.

"I guess he was pretty old," she said.

"Dad wasn't crying or anything."

"So?" she said.

"Do you think we'll go to a funeral? Shouldn't we be skipping school?"

"Why would we go to his funeral when we didn't go see him when he was alive?"

"But isn't that weird?" I said. "Can you imagine one of us not speaking to Mom or Dad forever? Can you imagine Mom not speaking to Grands and Gaggy?"

Julia started flipping through my CDs and video games, making sure I didn't have any of hers. "Grands and Gaggy are different," she said. "They love us. They're a part of our lives."

"Grandpa used to be part of ours," I said.

"You remember him?"

"He smelled like cigars and old magazines," I said. "He had a funny accent."

"He talked like a cabdriver." Julia giggled.

"He was kind of mean."

"He slept in long underwear and then wore it under his clothes the next day," Julia said.

"That's what you remember?"

"Well," she said. "It was pretty gross."

· · ·

I fell asleep playing Game Boy, and the next thing I knew it was morning. "Time to wake up," Dad was saying in his fake-cheerful voice. My pillow was so warm and soft on my cheek that in spite of his voice, I couldn't move.

"Come on, Michael," Dad said. "Mom has an early meeting. I have court, and I can't be late. And Mom says not to forget you're bringing the cello."

I rolled over and buried my head. When I was little, I used to wake up early and go find my parents in their room. Mom would roll over and say, "TV. Is. Now. Allowed." But Dad always got out of bed in his T-shirt and boxers and brought me into the dining room to read *Harry Potter*.

This is kind of embarrassing, but I sat in my dad's lap when we read together in the mornings until, like, fifth grade. On Friday nights when I was little, I'd wait for Dad to come back from the office, and he would pick me up and throw me in the air when he got home. He would make me an ice cream version of a protein shake, using combinations I could never believe, like strawberries and cornflakes, or bananas and carrots.

We don't do those things together anymore. "Whose jacket is this balled up in the corner of your room?" Dad said now. "Isn't this your school blazer that your mother spent three hundred dollars on? Why is it wet?"

I was going to explain about the water fight, but he'd already moved on to the corner of my room that back before winter vacation, my best friend Gus and I had turned into a prisoner of war camp for all of Julia's old American Girl dolls—Gus was taking pictures with his digital camera for a kind of photo-comic book he was making.

"This is sick," Dad said.

"It's been there for months," I started. "Me and Gus—"

"Gus and I!"

By the time he found my unfinished earth science report, I was sitting up. Dad lifted the poster board, and all the markers went sliding to the floor.

"Is this due today?" he said.

"Mom told me to go to bed. I was going to stay up and finish it, but she wouldn't let me."

"Honestly, Michael, you go to private school. You know how much that costs."

"But Grandpa died," I said. "That's why Mom said I should go to bed."

"Grandpa?" he said, as if he had no idea who I was talking about.

He was standing by the door to the bathroom, and I remembered how Julia had stood there last night while we talked about Grandpa. How she hadn't felt sad. How I hadn't felt sad either.

"You don't care about him," I spat out. I don't quite know what made me say that. I was surprised at how angry I sounded. I wasn't angry—not exactly. But what if Dad died? Would I feel sad? What if I was glad because then he wouldn't yell at me anymore? Or what if I died and Dad was like, "Michael died of a heart attack last night. I'm going to make myself a shake now."

My dad was staring at me, like he was still trying to figure out who I meant by "Grandpa." At that moment, I probably could have pretended that I hadn't said anything at all, and he would have gone along with it. But I didn't pretend. I said, "You don't even care that your own father died."

My dad's face turned white, then red.

Usually my dad has this way of not being surprised by anything I do. He reacts without missing a beat when he's mad. "Apologize to your mother." "Put that back!" "Sit down!" And, when he's really mad, "Go to your room." But now my dad didn't have anything ready to say. It wasn't that he looked puzzled. It was that he didn't look like anything. His face kind of froze.

And then, before he could unfreeze, something happened to the air between us.

By happened, I mean shimmered.

And by shimmered, I mean moved. The air between my dad and me actually twisted a little, the way air twists over pavement on a really hot day. My dad's long face blurred, his tie pushed itself into an S-curve, his knees moved several inches to the left of his legs.

At the same time, something touched me on the back of my neck. It felt like a needle. I slapped at it, but the feeling didn't go away. It was like getting a Novocain shot at the dentist. At first you're thinking, *This isn't so bad*, and then you've got tears in your eyes, and you're thinking, *Stop! Stop!*

"Ow!" I said. It was like my speaking broke the spell.

"What?" said my dad. "What was that?"

"There was something cold on my neck," I said. "And didn't you see the air move?"

"No," he said. But he shivered too. He shook his head as if to get rid of a sneeze, and then looked at his watch. "I want to see you in the shower in five minutes," he said. "And don't forget to eat something."

Chapter 2

Gus was in the kitchen before me, filling up his silver go-cup with coffee, milk, and four sugars. Gus has been drinking coffee since he was five, but it never stunted his growth. He's so much taller than me that one time he talked us into an R movie by saying that he was my babysitter. He eats breakfast with us every day because his mom leaves early for work, and it's embarrassing to still have a nanny, which he did until last year. His dad lives on the East Side with a new wife Gus calls Buffy even though her name is Helen.

"Oatmeal?" Gus said, raising his eyebrows.

Normally, you can't pay me to eat oatmeal. (Okay, I guess you can. One summer, my dad told me he'd give me five dollars for every bowl of oatmeal I ate, saying it would help me grow, and I ate two weeks' worth, bought an Xbox game, and never looked back.) Oatmeal, basically, is foul.

But now I wanted oatmeal the way I want pizza on a Friday night on the way to the movies. "I'm freezing," I said, which is weird because our apartment is so overheated you can wear shorts and a T-shirt when it's twenty below outside. "I think a nice bowl of oatmeal will warm me up. I want those little rivers."

"Rivers?"

"You know, how the brown sugar melts into little rivers before you add milk?"

Gus shook his head. He was around for the cash-for-oatmeal summer. He's been around for everything. He's been my best friend since he moved into my building in first grade.

Or at least he used to be. Last term he got pulled off the eighth-grade basketball team to play on varsity, and now he sits with the basketball team at lunch. Gus used to hate to go to East Hampton with his dad and Buffy on weekends, but now when they're out there, he plays basketball with Trip Hall, who is a sophomore, and whose family has so much money that even after his dad went to prison for insider trading, they still have a beach house with two swimming pools, and a big apartment on Eighty-eighth Street, right around the corner from school. Gus hangs out in that apartment now after practice, and he gets invited to parties there. On Valentine's Day, Siobhan Clarke, a girl in tenth grade who is one of Trip's friends, sent Gus a carnation with the message: "Guess who?" Here's what I got at school on Valentine's Day: a carnation from Gus with a card that said, "You owe me two dollars for the flower." Ha-ha.

Sometimes I wish Gus wasn't funny. Then maybe it wouldn't be so bad that he's slowly stopping being friends with me.

He put his hand into the box of chocolate crunch cereal. "Since when do you eat oatmeal?" he said.

"Since now," I muttered. I mutter a lot to Gus these days. I don't want to talk to Gus about his ditching me at school—it's too embarrassing. But it's hard for me not to act like I'm mad at him for no reason.

"I thought you hated it."

"Did you know my grandpa died?" I said.

"Grands? Oh my gosh."

"No, the other one."

Dad started bellowing from the hall, "Okay everyone, it's time to go!"

"I didn't even know you had another grandpa," Gus said.

"Well, I did."

"Well, I'm sorry."

"Let's go!" shouted Dad. He sounded normal, but he looked kind of weird. Pale. His hair was messed up, like he'd run his hand through it and hadn't smoothed it back down.

Gus grabbed his coffee and headed for the hall. I still had to brush my teeth and my hair, which, when I caught a glimpse of it in the microwave door, was ridiculous. I wear my curly hair long because it stands up on top of my head and makes me look taller. But my dad is right about it. Today I could've been Ronald McDonald, except with brown hair instead of red. And I hadn't had time to take a single bite of oatmeal.

By the time I rushed into our front hall, where the elevator comes, carrying my half-finished earth science poster, my book bag, my cello, and the oatmeal that I'd decided I would try to eat in the cab, my dad was holding the elevator door, and Gus and Julia were waiting inside. Julia's hair was slicked back, her shoulders straight under the backpack that holds all her important fat textbooks that she has no problem remembering to bring home every day, a fact my dad reminds me of constantly. I noticed for the first time that Gus had grown taller than Julia. How could he keep growing and growing, while I never budged past five feet?

Just as I was having that thought, I heard the high-pitched screeching that is supposed to let you know it's time to close the elevator door. The annoying sound coupled with the annoying cold feeling made me feel, well, annoyed. How was I going to get away from this? I wanted to put my hands up to block my ears, but my hands were full—I'd slung the cello strap over my shoulder, the poster board was rolled up under my arm, I was carrying my book bag in one hand, and I'd balanced the bowl of oatmeal in the palm of the other. I tried lifting the arm holding the oatmeal up to my face. Great idea, right?

The bowl slipped instantly out of my hands, and hit the tile floor, breaking—duh—down the middle. As oatmeal oozed into the cracks between the tiles, my backpack, which had fallen next to it, started to get wet. I was stepping on the earth science poster board, and the cello strap had slipped down my arm and was digging into the inside of my elbow. The elevator had moved from screeching to a bleating sound that reminds me of the foghorn they blow at soccer games when Gus has scored so many goals they're sending kids like me in for substitutions. My head was pounding. My dad's eyes traveled from the oatmeal on the floor to my face. "Court," he said. "I have to be in court."

Why was I getting so cold?

"Will. Someone," I shouted. "Stop. That. Infernal. Noise."

Everybody stared. It was the yelling. I don't really yell. And the word "infernal." I guess no one expected me to know what it meant. Now that I think about it, I don't.

After a second, Julia and Gus stepped out of the elevator. The doors closed and the clanging stopped. Julia said, "I'll get a towel," and ran for the kitchen. Gus said, "Here," and lifted my cello from my shoulder and set it down by the elevator door. I was still really cold, but having the cello moved was a big help.

"I have something of importance to impart to you," I heard myself whisper to my dad when Gus's back was turned. Of importance? To impart? These weren't real words. They were vocabulary. "I'm going to leave home someday," I hissed. "And you're going to spend the rest of your life wondering if you could have loved me more. The question will keep you alive. And the question will kill you. Are you prepared for that?"

My dad's small brown eyes grew large. It was almost painful to look at him. But I was distracted by the cold feeling that was getting worse. And by the fact that I had no idea what I was saying. What does "impart" even mean?

But I didn't have time to think about the strangeness of what I said, because now the cold was growing extreme. Was there a window open? Was the cold coming from the elevator? I felt like I was standing near something dangerous. Maybe the elevator was a giant tunnel of cold, and I could get sucked into it if I took so much as a step toward it.

"Michael," my dad started, but before he could continue, Julia was crouching down between us to wipe up the oatmeal, and Gus was picking up my earth science poster board from the floor. "Michael," my dad said again, but the moment had passed—his voice had lost its I'm-figuring-it-out tone, and gone back to a you're-in-trouble tone. He grabbed the poster from Gus with one hand, and my elbow with the other. "Downstairs," he said. "Now." His cheeks were burning bright red, like Julia's when she danced Cinderella even though she had the flu.

Dad was still holding my arm while George the doorman hailed our cab. "No Xbox," Dad said through gritted teeth. "No Game Boy. No allowance. No TV. I don't know what is going on with you today, but I've just about had it. This is my house, and if nothing else, you will respect me in it."

"But Dad—," I started. I wanted to tell him that I was freezing, that it wasn't my fault, that I took back what I'd said. I wanted to tell him he hadn't said anything about Grandpa. But as soon as he let go of my elbow, I felt myself beginning to warm—a little. I slipped into the backseat of the cab between Gus and Julia, feeling warmer still. My dad slid the cello across our three laps and closed the door without saying good-bye.

"What is going on?" said Julia as the cab shot forward one block and stopped at a red light. "Michael, are you okay?" I looked straight out in front of me. I didn't want to explain what I'd said to my dad, those strange words that didn't feel like something I'd been thinking. I wanted to wait to talk until the cold feeling went away completely.

But it didn't. The road through the park dipped down into a trench that cuts through the sunny green lawns of the park. All we could see out of the cab windows were old stone walls on either side, and above us, the bare branches of trees, and a low, gray sky. I clenched my teeth to keep them from chattering.

Chapter 3

Mr. Morton, the drama teacher, was moderating first-period study hall, drinking coffee out of a paper cup as tall as his forearm was long. He waved the cup in my direction. "Favor us, Michael," he said, in the fake English accent he uses to read Shakespeare plays aloud, "with at least the appearance of industry." I pulled out my earth science poster, which had gotten crushed in the taxi, and started coloring.

My project looked worse than I remembered. It was supposed to show the layers of stuff on the inside of planet earth. Except the circle I had drawn for the earth looked more like an oval on one end, and a rectangle on the other—I'd kind of realized it wasn't much of a circle halfway through drawing it, and tried to backtrack, which turned out to be even more of a disaster.

I was coloring the mantle red, and the red marker was running out. No matter how hard I pressed, I ended up with only a thin stripe of color that disappeared almost entirely when I accidentally rubbed it with my arm. At this point all I could do was make it look like at least I'd *tried* to color.

But there's something about just doing the same thing over

and over that always makes me feel better. Like, on the first day that Gus didn't save me a seat at lunch—when I walked into the cafeteria to find him at the basketball table, hunched over because I'm sure he didn't want to see me looking for him—I went home after school and just started playing *Wreckless: The Yakuza Missions*. It was weird, by the time I'd gotten through three levels, I kind of didn't care anymore about Gus. I didn't feel better, exactly. I guess I just didn't *feel*. My whole brain was filled up with remembering all the details of exactly how hard to push the buttons, exactly when to move my guy and how far.

I started to think about *The Yakuza Missions* as I was coloring, and about video games in general, and it started to hit me that the layers of the earth were kind of like the levels of a video game. They get weirder and you know less about what you're getting into as you move to the center, and there are these little extra hard parts in between.

Like D-double-prime. It's this thin ring around the iron ball in the very middle of the earth. No one really knows what is inside D-double-prime, or why the sound waves made by earthquakes can't get through it. Crazy, right?

It's funny how quickly I can get into a daydream, because after what felt like no time at all, the bell rang, and there I was just barely done with the iron core. D-double-prime looked nothing like the way I'd imagined it—it was just a whole bunch of green squiggly lines. My red marker was totally kaput, and I still had to finish coloring in the mantle. Not to mention the entire crust of the earth. We have four minutes between classes, and I was supposed to be drawing all the oceans and land masses of our planet. In cross section. There was just no way.

So instead of coloring the crust, I decided to leave the outline of the egg shape, and just label everything. But even then I miscalculated how much space the words would take up, and ended up kind of crunching the letters at the end of "basaltic magma," and "Mohorovicic Discontinuity." My poster looked like a three-year-old had done it, like something Mr. Blum was going to write "See me" on, because what he had to say was too harsh to put in writing.

At the sound of the second bell, I rushed out of study hall and ran up the stairs to the instrument room. The instrument room is on the top floor of the school, across the hall from the upper-class lounge. Every time I have orchestra, I have to push past the stream of older kids on their way to the lounge. I hunch over to keep the cello from bouncing on the steps, and the older kids plaster themselves against the wall so I don't hit them with the big black case. It's totally embarrassing.

Today I passed Gus's new best friend, Trip Hall. Trip Hall doesn't know that I'm Gus's old best friend. I don't think he really has any idea *who* I am, except the really short eighth grader with the really big cello. "Look," he said, when he saw me now. "It's Quasimodo." Siobhan Clarke and Torrance Hisslin were right behind him, and they giggled. All three of them had to line up against the wall so I could pass by. Julia used to be friends with Siobhan and Torrance, but not anymore. "They've turned into bimbos," I remember hearing Julia tell my mom.

Trip said, "What do you have in there, a dead body?" Siobhan and Torrance giggled again. The way I felt as they watched me hitch the cello down one step at a time reminded me of a thin kind of papery crunching noise, like I'd sat on a bag of potato chips in the middle of a quiet room.

But I felt something else as well. The cold feeling—it got worse. It had never really gone away, but now it was like a tingling—like the way your hands feel in the winter when you've been back inside for a while, but they're still a little numb.

Usually when kids make comments about the cello, or about how short I am, it makes me feel small. But today I felt kind of—I don't know—mad. Like the coldness was waking me up—making me see things. Like I wasn't the kid being made fun of, but I was watching that kid.

I didn't do anything about it, though. Just looked down at the ground like a big wuss. And got to orchestra after everyone else was done tuning, so my notes sounded worse than usual. At the end of orchestra, Mr. Pierce gave me a lecture on the importance of being on time, and I was even more late for earth science. At least I had something I could turn in. That would be a relief.

Except that as soon as I walked through the classroom door, I noticed that Tori Lublin was standing up at the front of the room, holding a plasticine model of a volcano. I watched in horror as Mr. Blum plugged in a cord that came from the bottom of her volcano, and a red lightbulb inside it turned on and smoke started to rise from the crater.

Please, please, please, I prayed inside my head. We're not really religious in my family—my dad was Jewish but is now an atheist, and my mom was Christian but likes the Jewish holidays better. No one ever taught me how to pray, and I've just started making up my own way of doing it, primarily in moments of great need, like this one. "Please, please, please—" is generally as far as I get.

"Excuse me, Tori," said Mr. Blum. "I see we have a late entrant. Please take a seat, Michael, so that Tori can continue her oral report."

"Oral?" I said. My prayer had definitely not been answered.

"You do remember that today we're presenting our oral reports?"

I swallowed hard. I found my seat. I tried not to cry. No, I did not remember.

This didn't make any sense, but I started to be a little mad at the cold feeling, as if it was responsible for my forgetting. Why wasn't it going away? It made everything else that was annoying so much worse. Usually, I guess I'm pretty good at ignoring things. But the cold feeling was waking me up, and making me see. I didn't like it.

Meanwhile, Tori started to explain how most volcanoes happen under the ocean without anyone knowing about them. Is it worth mentioning that Tori's dad is a movie producer, and one of his assistants helps her with her homework every night? It's true.

Gus went next, standing up slowly, untangling the sleeves of his blazer—we are supposed to wear blazers all the time but can mostly get away with carrying them.

When he took off his shoes, all the girls were like, "Eww!"

His shoes are falling apart, and he has wrapped the left one in duct tape. He put the shoes on Mr. Blum's desk, on either side of a rubber place mat that I recognized from his kitchen.

For a second, he leaned over the place mat, scratching the back of his knee with his opposite foot, a habit he has. He pushed down on the shoes and moved them toward each other, and the place mat was forced up into a mountain. He made the simple motion look like a magic trick.

"My shoes are the plates that move around on the surface of the earth," he said. "And this place mat is showing how mountains are formed."

"Well conceived," Mr. Blum commented. "If slightly unhygienic."

Brilliant Ewan Greer went next, and we had to turn out the lights so he could display the computer modeling he'd done of the formation of the Appalachian mountain range. It was basically the same as Gus's project, except it looked like something developed by NASA, instead of developed by Gus on the way out the door that morning.

Ewan didn't come to Selden until just before winter break, but even if he had started at the beginning of the year, he wouldn't have fit in. He doesn't play sports because of his asthma. He's on a scholarship. He wears shirts that look shiny, and pants that are too short. He doesn't wash his hair. He reads during lunch. And he's always sticking his hand up like he is dying to tell everyone the answers. Even the teachers are annoyed and don't want to call on him.

At the end of the presentation, he showed a picture of himself on top of some of the mountains in the Appalachian range, and in the picture, he actually looked clean and healthy. He was standing next to a man in a big sweater and a red ski hat, and they were both smiling big goofy smiles.

"I took that picture with the timer on my camera," Ewan said.

"Is that your dad?" Mr. Blum asked.

Even in the dim light, I could see that Ewan was ducking his head. "Yeah," he mumbled, and switched off the projector. "It's an old picture. That was a really long time ago."

He sounded embarrassed, which is kind of weird. I know his parents are divorced, because only his mom is listed in the school directory, and that's what they do at Selden. But I don't know why that would be embarrassing. Half the kids in our class have parents who are divorced.

Sam Gershwin went next. All he had to show for himself was his sister's garnet ring—the melted rock inside the earth's mantle is made up of the same stuff that's in garnet. When Mr. Blum asked him if it was okay to pass the ring around the classroom, Sam got really nervous. "Okay," he said. "But don't lose it. She doesn't exactly know it's here." Sam's lame report made me feel better, but then again, everybody knows Sam goes to Study Skills, which means he spends study hall in a small room in the basement where a lady teaches you how to make neat outlines of everything. Study Skills doesn't help anyone, it just makes it official that you're dumb. My mom thinks I need to go.

Every time Mr. Blum asked for a volunteer, I looked down. My only chance of survival was hoping there wasn't enough time for all the presentations in one day. Everything would be better if I had one more day. The cold feeling was like having to pee—always there, getting a little worse with the passing of time. Maybe, after I warmed up, I could ask Julia what she did in earth science when she was in eighth grade. She probably got an A. I couldn't help thinking about how warm her room would be right now.

"Michael?" Mr. Blum was sitting on the corner of his desk, brushing off the spot where Gus's shoes had left some caked mud. "I think you're the last one."

When I looked under my desk for the poster board, I realized it had unrolled. I had been stepping on it all during class without realizing it, and now, on top of being really sucky, it was covered with black footprints.

"Um," I said, standing in front of the whole class, with my half-finished, stepped-on, wrinkled poster stretched between two hands. I wanted to rub my hands together to warm up my fingers, but I was holding the poster. Mr. Blum rolled his palm open, indicating that I should start talking.

"This is, I guess," I said, "the earth? These are the layers." I couldn't think of anything else to say. Not another word. I *was* dumb. I was the stupidest person in the world.

"Do you want to tell us a little bit *about* the layers?" Mr. Blum prompted. "Or at least do you want to tell us how your report takes the information you got from the book and goes a little further?"

"I didn't know this was going to be an out-loud kind of thing," I said.

"You don't have to say anything extraordinary, Michael. Just tell us a little bit about what you had in mind here."

"Um," I started again. I pointed to the center of the egg-shaped orb that was supposed to be earth. "This is the core." I pointed to the half-colored pinkish red section. "This is the mantle. I don't know what else I'm supposed to say about them. The mantle is hot. The iron is really, um, iron-y."

Mr. Blum sighed. "Try to expand these ideas a little?"

Expand this, I was thinking. If I brought home another C, my dad was going to throw the Xbox away. Thinking about the Xbox made me start thinking about video games, and thinking about video games reminded me of the idea I'd had while I was coloring that morning in study hall. And even though the cold feeling was really annoying, it was also keeping me awake in a weird way. I think it was making my brain work differently. Was my brain working faster? I don't know. But it was the cold feeling—I swear—that made me start talking.

"What this really shows," I said, "is not just the layers of the earth. But a map for a new video game. The name of the video game is D-double-prime. D-double-prime is here." I pointed to the green squiggles I'd made outside the circle of iron at the core. "It's that weird layer you were talking about the other day that no one understands, even actual scientists. But the game starts here." I pointed to the top of the crust. "You need to get all the way through the crust and the mantle. You have to go down there because there's a war going on at the surface of the planet, and you're fighting against the computer machines who are taking over from the humans. The only way to shut them down is to get some kind of special rock that's inside that layer."

"It would have to be iron," Mr. Blum said. "The core is made of iron. Didn't you just explain that?"

"Okay," I said. "Some special iron. And you start off fighting the machines, until you can find the hole into the deep parts of the crust."

"Like an abandoned mine?"

"Yeah," I said. "And then you get into the mantle from there. You have to get on a special kind of wet suit that would allow you to swim through the melted rock."

"That would be some wet suit," said Mr. Blum. But he was giving me a look he usually saves for students who do the homework.

"Or you can go in a special submarine kind of thing, with blasters to fight off all the scary dinosaur slug things that you find in the mine or the mantle or whatever. Things would be catching fire, like, constantly."

"That's actually a really cool idea," I heard Ewan say.

"I'd play it," said Sam.

"The first geology-based video game," Mr. Blum said.

"The last level would be D-double-prime," I went on, feeling my own idea growing as I thought about it. "And down there it would be, like, totally black, except you'd see pieces of the earth that had sunk down there, like on the news when there's a flood somewhere and you see people's roofs and cars and trees floating down a river. Except a lot of it would be on fire. You'd see water lit up only by the flames."

"You realize, of course, that by the time pieces of the earth's crust reached D-double-prime, all traces of human life would have been completely obliterated?" said Mr. Blum.

"But this is a video game," I protested. "It has to be cool."

"Okay," said Mr. Blum, putting a hand in the air. "I stand corrected."

Just then the bell rang. Everyone started piling up their books and shuffling their papers together. I felt kind of excited by my idea, and I was thinking about asking Mr. Blum right then and there if he could promise I wasn't going to get a C. But before I could even ask the question, he said, "Michael, can you see me for a second?"

Mr. Blum gestured for me to take a seat at an empty desk in the front row. "Your video game idea was great," he said. "It showed a good understanding of the material and I think even helped the class find the magic in what we know about the interior of our planet. But when I look at your work on the page, I have to wonder why we don't see any of your good ideas coming through."

I wasn't sure if I was supposed to try to answer that question.

"You can do better," Mr. Blum said. That's what teachers are always saying to me. "But there's nothing I can do to help you if you don't start to pay attention. Leave yourself more time. And here, I'll give you a chance now. If you want to bring this home and turn it into a real map of a video game, I'll let you turn it in by Friday. How's that?"

"Okay," I said, feeling all the excitement of people actually liking my idea flow out of my body. I didn't want another chance with that poster board. I was too cold to work on anything. All I wanted was to get warm. Playing video games would warm me up, not coloring in maps of them. I didn't care that I was crushing my poster as I rolled it back up and stuck it in the top of my book bag. The second bell rang, and Mr. Blum said, "Better hurry, Michael. You're not supposed to be late for assembly. Good luck."

I ran, but still, I got to assembly when everyone else was sitting down, and I had to stand looking for a place to sit for far too long. It's been weeks since I would expect Gus to be saving me a seat, but I always kind of check anyway, like one day things will go back to normal. I noticed Julia was all comfy in her seat already. She was sitting next to the exchange student from Germany, Inge. Because she's so busy with ballet, Julia always makes friends with the exchange students. Every time they go back to wherever they've come from—and some of these places, I've never even heard of—Julia boo-hoos to my mom about how she has no friends at school, until my parents pay for the plane ticket to go visit them. It's so unfair. They give me a hard time about each and every Xbox game, and in the meantime, Julia's spending thousands of dollars on international flights. Last summer alone, she flew to Japan *and* Buenos Aires. The other day, I heard her tell Mom that London was getting boring.

I must have been looking around for a long time, because

31

eventually Ms. Rosoff beckoned me to her. Ms. Rosoff's the art teacher who isn't really a teacher at all—or even an artist. She did an assembly once where she told us she was some kind of handwriting expert who used to work for the FBI. No one believed her—last time I checked, FBI agents don't wear big purple dresses and talk so softly into the microphone that you can't hear half of what they say. Near the end of her assembly, everyone at Selden started clapping as if she were finished, and we had to write her personal letters of apology that were signed by our parents.

Anyway, Ms. Rosoff is my advisor, and it's her job to make sure everyone in her group shows up for assembly and checks in with her. Usually she doesn't even do this—she's the kind of teacher who never knows when the girls are passing notes and can't remember which period we have lunch. But this morning, she pointed out a free seat in the front row, right next to Ewan Greer.

Ewan carries a giant duffel instead of a backpack, and he slid it over on the floor to make room. Ewan always keeps that duffel bag with him, as if he's afraid someone will take it. Which they probably would, because he's Ewan, the kid who breaks every curve. "Hi," Ewan said. I lifted my hand in a half wave and he flinched, like he was afraid that I was going to hit him. "I liked your video game idea."

"Un-huh," I said. With kids like Ewan, it's scary to say hi to them. You don't want to be the only person in the world to be their friend.

But then I made the mistake of looking Ewan straight in the eye. The cold that I'd been feeling all morning suddenly got much worse. Looking at Ewan, I felt how cold he was, and I felt as cold as that. I felt like I *was* Ewan. Inside his small gray eyes, I was standing on a blacktop mountain road. I recognized the road, because in art, it is the only thing Ewan ever draws. I'd seen it in charcoal, and papier-mâché. I'd seen it wrapping around the outside of a coil pot, the tall pine trees etched with a paper clip, the rock cliff that drops off to one side imprinted with old toothbrush bristles.

I was so cold, I couldn't think of the word "cold." Instead, I was thinking that I was locked. I couldn't move.

As I continued to stare at Ewan, I think he was starting to get a little freaked out. He attempted a smile, but all I could see were his eyes, and behind them that lonely, curving road. I saw Ewan walking alongside it. Snow fell down the collar of his jacket—I felt how it would be on his neck. The sky was gray. Just as I could feel the cold wind along the side of the road, I could feel Ewan's wishing, wishing for something he knew he couldn't have. And I was wishing very hard too.

I heard these words come out of my mouth: "Your dad was watching you," I said. "That day when you stood by the road. He knew what you wanted. He wanted it too. But all he could do was watch. He's watching you now."

I swear I had no idea why I said that to him. I didn't know what I was talking about.

Ewan's smile sagged, without disappearing entirely, as if he was so surprised by what I'd said he'd forgotten about his own face entirely.

"What did you say?" he said.

"Nothing," I said, and I found I could move my eyes again. "Forget it."

"Forget it?" he kind of choked out. His eyes were wet, and his voice was cracking. Was he crying?

"Shh," I said, because you don't want to have people see you crying in assembly. You don't want to be noticed in assembly at all.

Ewan stood up, threaded his way through the legs of everyone in our row, and walked up the aisle to the doors in the back as if he didn't care that everyone was staring at him, and that you couldn't just walk out of assembly without getting a detention.

I turned to see if anyone else had noticed, and my eyes bumped right into Ms. Rosoff's watery blue ones, which always remind me of a fish's. She must have heard the whole thing.

"What did you say to him?" she whispered. "You made him cry."

"Me?" I whispered back. "Nothing. I don't know. Isn't he going to get in trouble? He's leaving assembly."

"You said something about his father," Ms. Rosoff hissed. Her face was so close to mine now, I could smell toothpaste on her breath—she smokes, but no one is supposed to know—and I suddenly remembered how during her handwriting assembly there was this one cool moment when she took anonymous handwriting samples from kids and could tell all sorts of things about them based on the size of their letters, or the way they cross their *t*'s. Because my writing goes downhill, she told me I was shy. She said she suspected Gus had divorced parents because he didn't close his *o*'s at the top. Everyone who was being rude in the audience suddenly got quiet, and for a few minutes, it was like, "Wow, maybe this isn't the same person who gets lost on the way to the teachers' lounge."

"What did you say to Ewan?" Ms. Rosoff asked again, and she didn't seem lost at all. She seemed angry. "About his father."

"I didn't say it," I insisted. I thought for a second about telling her how cold I was, how the cold feeling was getting worse. "I don't know anything about his father."

"You don't know," she spat out, in that I-have-a-hard-time-believing-this voice, "that Ewan's father died in a car crash a month before he moved here?"

"Oh," I said. Before I even remembered what I'd said to Ewan, I thought, *Oh, man. Poor Ewan.* And then I made the connection: Ewan's dad. Ewan's gray eyes. Ewan's road.

"Ms. Rosoff," I said, "I think I need to go to the nurse."

Chapter 4

"You do sound a little hoarse," said Mrs. Meade, the school nurse, when I told her about the chills.

She leaned back in her worn desk chair, which had a child's block taped onto one of the legs where a wheel was missing. Her office was in the basement, and she had filled it with fake plants and the lace doilies she crocheted when there weren't any sick kids around. I used to love to go see Mrs. Mead. She treats the little kids like they're puppies, rubbing their foreheads and stuffing them with lemon drops that are supposedly some kind of medicine. She always has Kool-Aid in her mini-fridge, and she doles it out in Dixie cups decorated with stupid knock-knock jokes, like, "Eileen who? Ei-leen-over to tie my shoe." But after you're in fourth grade, she treats you like an ex-con—to get any kind of sympathy from her at all, you have to throw up or have a fever.

Until last year, when a kid in Julia's class had hallucinations in the lunchroom and his parents sued the school. Apparently, he had been writing about the voices in his head for months in the journal he was keeping in his English class and going to Mrs.

Meade twice a week to complain of headaches. She'd thought he was faking. Ever since then, Mrs. Meade sends kids home at the first hint of sickness.

"There's a chance you're coming down with a cold," she mused again, "and if you're coming down with a cold, then you're most certainly contagious. I'm going to call your mother. I think you should see your *family doctor* right away. In fact, I'm going to type you up a little note that I'll keep a copy of right here in my file."

Since my mother was in a meeting, her secretary told Mrs. Meade it was okay for me to go home in a car service by myself, which is something you can do only if your parents sign about twenty-five forms in the first week of school. In the car, I decided that as soon as I got home, I would fix myself a peanut butter and Fluff sandwich, and go back to playing *Midtown Madness*. Definitely not *Aliens Versus Predator: Extinction*. *Aliens Versus Predator: Extinction* is new, and I was already feeling a little light-headed, and kind of lost in the way you feel in the beginning of a video game, when you keep falling off the same cliff.

I was still really cold. I'd zipped my jacket up to my chin and crossed my arms in front of my chest, but it wasn't helping. Maybe peanut butter and Fluff would help. But as soon as I got home and took a bite of my sandwich, I spat it back into the sink and tossed the rest of the sandwich into the trash. It was the sugar. Somehow, mixed with the cold, it hurt my teeth. My mom can't drink cold water first thing in the morning—she says it makes her fillings hurt, and that's how I felt now, like there was a shooting pain from the outside of my teeth traveling into my gums and then straight into the bones of my jaw. Was it my fillings? I don't have fillings. What was going on with me?

Inside the fridge, I found leftover creamed spinach. Creamed spinach usually makes me retch. But now I took the container of it over to the microwave. As soon as it started to cook and I could smell the rich, creamy bitterness, I knew it was exactly what I was in the mood for.

When it was hot, I put as much in my mouth as I could. It was slippery and slimy and I could taste the part of it that always made me gag, the part that tastes the way the grass smells in the spring in the park. But at the same time, it melted on my tongue almost like chocolate, and the gritty parts of it didn't bother me.

After I'd finished the spinach and licked the bowl—licked it!—I felt good, but only for just a second. I sighed, and as soon as I inhaled that big sigh back in, I was cold again.

"A good smoke," I heard myself say out loud. A smoke? I don't smoke. If my mom caught me smoking, she would kill me. She likes to say "I want to catch you stealing before I catch you smoking." But I wanted a cigar—not even a cigarette!—so much that I didn't care how much trouble I would get into if I got caught. I went back into the front hall to put on my coat and go out to find a place that would sell cigars to a thirteen-year-old who looks like he's nine.

What was wrong with me? I wondered for a second if I should tell a grown-up. But if I told a grown-up, I wouldn't be able to get a cigar. And I had to have one. Right away.

In our front hall, the wall across from the elevator is covered in mirrors. It's very hard to walk past it and not catch a glimpse of yourself. Julia spends hours staring at her reflection here. But on my way to get a cigar, I caught a glimpse in the mirror of something that made me stop. When I turned for a second look, I was expecting to find staring back at me nothing more than my own reflection. But my own reflection—my frizzed-out hair, my untucked shirt—was gone. This totally blew my mind, but I swear it was true. My reflection—me—I wasn't there.

It took me a second to see what was in the mirror in my place: an old man. His white hair was cut short, and his eyebrows were bushy. He wasn't fat, like Santa Claus. He was thin and looked strong. He was dressed in a plaid wool shirt and jeans that looked like they were about to go in the knees. He was smiling a little too intensely, like someone who has been hit on the head with a shovel.

It was Grandpa. Grandpa-who-was-dead.

I closed my eyes and opened them again, waiting for the vision to go away.

But Grandpa was still there. He turned when I turned. When I stared again, he stared. I lifted my left hand. He lifted his right. I waved. He waved at the same exact time. I could look down and see my own self, but when I looked into the mirror, the old man was me.

I felt like one of those guys in a cartoon who runs over a cliff edge and then hangs in the air with his legs moving. I was thinking, *If this doesn't go away pretty soon, I'm going to have to start thinking it's real.*

I walked up close to the mirror and looked at the man there—Grandpa. I really looked, the way you stare into your own eyes, wondering how other people see you. *Go away,* I was thinking. *Now it is time for this to start making sense,* I thought. But it didn't make sense.

And then the cold got worse. Not a little worse. Or a slow worse. A really fast, bad worse, like suddenly, the cold I'd been feeling before was actually warmth and this new, unbearable, sharp pain was redefining what it meant to be cold. The new cold had come from the inside of Grandpa—the bloodshot whites of his eyes. The second I looked into them, the cold in my chest suddenly spread, like an explosion into my shoulders, down my arms, through my hips, to my toes and then back up. The cold pounded against the inside of my forehead. It clogged my ears. I couldn't seem to take a breath. When I tried to look down, I found I couldn't move my eyes. They were locked on to Grandpa's.

"Stop it," I said, though it was hard to move my lips. "Let go." And then—because I didn't have time to figure out if I should try not to panic or just beg, I begged. "Please," I said. "Please, please, please."

The cold feeling had moved all the way down to my feet. I could hardly feel them, and it was like they were getting heavier, like I was being pulled down. I pedaled my arms, gasping, kicking my feet to try to make them grab on to the floor, but the floor was feeling strangely un-solid. There was no one to call for help. My parents were at work, and Julia wouldn't get home from school and ballet for hours.

"Help!" I begged Grandpa in the mirror. He wouldn't let go of my eyes. "Let me go." He just stared.

I felt my legs disappearing. I was sinking into a current of dark air that was so cold it was thick, like water right before it starts to freeze. Moving down faster and faster, I struggled against what was pulling me in. I couldn't see.

Mr. Blum once told us that when you step outside in the Arctic, it takes one minute to get frostbite, which is your skin freezing so badly it dies. It wasn't my skin I was concerned with. It was my bones. I was so cold I worried they were going to crack.

It's funny, in video games when you die, it's not that big a deal. Sometimes it's even funny, like when a voice comes on that says, "Yay, you win . . . not!" or when blood and guts spill out of the fighter you're playing. I'd never for a second in my life thought I was in any danger of dying for real. Until now. It was different. It was scary. All I wanted was to go back to my life. I didn't care anymore that I wasn't like Gus, that Julia always won. I wasn't mad at my dad. I could see in one big rush that I had the best, easiest, happiest life in the world. I wanted it back—Julia, Gus, my dad. My mom. I wanted everything to stay exactly the same as it had always been. I wasn't ready.

Chapter 5

I don't remember what happened next. I think I might have passed out from the pain and the cold. I woke up lying on my back.

At least I could breathe again. For a few moments I lay still, just enjoying it, but it's amazing how quickly you can start to take breathing for granted. Where was I? Underneath me was a hard, cold floor. Was it the tiles of our foyer? No. As I touched it, I could tell it was smoother, and harder.

When I sat up, I saw that I was in a long corridor. Was it a school? The walls were lined with sets of lockers and oak doors with frosted glass windows. I smelled chalk and formaldehyde, which made me think of the high school science rooms at Selden.

"Michael!" The voice came from behind me, and even without having heard it in so long, I knew it was Grandpa's. I turned, and there he was, crouching down behind me, his back to a locker.

Up close, he looked awful. His eyelids drooped. His fingers were knobby. I couldn't tell if what was wrong with him was because he was a lot older than the last time I'd seen him, or because he was actually dead, but there was a blue tint to his skin, and his hair was thin, like if I pulled it, it would come out.

Grandpa reached out a hand and touched my cheek. Sort of. I could see his hand there, but where he was touching me, I only felt a shock of cold, as if he were holding an ice cube to my skin. Then he sat down, leaning against the locker behind him, drawing his knees up to his chest.

"Where am I?" I managed to say. "Why are you here? Am I—?"

Grandpa knitted his eyebrows together. "I am dead," he said. "But you are very much alive."

"Thank you," I breathed in the same direction that I usually prayed my "please, please, please" prayer. But did I believe him? If I was alive, and he was dead, how come we were talking?

Grandpa took a deep breath in through his nose, like he was smelling something really good. I don't know if it was just my imagination, but his skin turned pink—or at least a little less blue—as he breathed in. He looked better.

"That feels beauteous," he said, taking another deep breath. "I've been wanting to do that for—well, I have no idea. Try that, take a deep, deep breath."

I did what he said, but for me, the air was just . . . air. "You haven't said where we are," I said. "And can you please explain what happened?"

"I wish I could answer your questions," Grandpa said. "But I'm not sure I understand what's happening any better than you do." He breathed deeply through his nose again. "The air smells sweet to me," he added. "Positively sweet."

I took a breath myself. Still nothing.

"One minute it smells like cherry-flavored medicine," Grandpa said. "And the next, it's like lemon. The tart and sweet filling in a lemon meringue pie."

I was starting to wonder how I would get back, and all Grandpa could do was talk about pie.

"So you don't know anything about what's going on here?" I said. "About how come I got so cold? Aren't you here to rescue me?"

Grandpa was turning his head to see what I looked like from different angles as if he were a photographer lining up a shot. "I didn't come to rescue you, Michael," he said. "I'm afraid that you rescued me." I didn't quite know what to make of that comment. How had I rescued him? All I'd done was get so cold I must have passed out. And somehow found myself in a place I'd never been.

Was this really my *grandpa?* It was impossible, of course, but on the other hand, I could see him with my own eyes. I remembered him. And even if I hadn't, I could hear my mom's and dad's and Julia's voices wrapped up inside the fibers of his voice. He leaned on his words the same way, a way I didn't even know my own family did until I heard it coming from Grandpa now.

"This doesn't make sense," I said.

"I know," said Grandpa. "And yet, I feel so good. I feel so happy to be here. To be with you. There's something about your eyes," he said softly. "You have your grandmother's eyes, and yet . . ." He squinted. "You've turned out looking exactly like your mother in every other way. Your sister, she's the one who always looked like our side."

"You don't look like Julia," I said, though even as I said it, I realized he did. Julia is tall and narrow—her jaw is long, and her eyes are a little hooded. Grandpa had a lot of the same shapes in his face.

"You've already seen it," Grandpa said, and I sat up straighter.

"You can read my mind?"

"Only a little. But that's not because I'm dead. Or even because I'm your grandfather. Everyone can do that. It's funny, how people convince themselves they can't."

"I don't understand," I said.

"But you do! When we're alive we convince ourselves we don't understand things when we do."

"This is freaking me out," I said. "I don't believe that you're dead, and you're here. And we're talking."

"I don't believe it either," Grandpa said. "But you know what? I don't care. I want to be here."

I looked away from Grandpa. There was something kind of blinding about him. I didn't know if it was his personality or if it was the unrealness of the situation. I needed a break, and I looked away.

The hallway had started to fill with students. They looked almost like grown-ups, except they were dressed in clothes that were tight in some strange places, and puffy in others. None of them seemed to notice us, sitting on the floor. "You have no idea where we are?" I asked.

"No, I do," said Grandpa. "That question, at least, I can answer. We're at Baruch College. My mind must have traveled here after seeing you today, at your school. I never know where I'm going to end up."

"What do you mean, traveled? End up?"

But Grandpa had gotten distracted by a group of soldiers in heavy black shoes and light brown shirts walking past us. Seeing the soldiers, the girls laughed. "C Company." Grandpa snorted. "I know those guys. Irish."

"Why can't they see us? Why is everyone wearing those costumes?"

"Those aren't costumes," Grandpa said. He was answering me as if I were interrupting him watching a movie, giving me the shortest possible answers so he wouldn't miss anything. "This was 1951. I know because your grandmother"—he pointed to the cluster of girls who were still giggling—"is still wearing her hair long."

"That's Grandma?" I said. "This is your college? Where are the dorms?"

"I lived at home," he said. "In the Bronx. I was in the army back then. It was a paycheck and a chance to go to college. Though not a fancy one—this is Baruch, part of City College. You know City College?"

I didn't.

"Oy," he said. "Your father goes away to an elite school, and his son never even knows there could be another way."

The girl with long hair who was supposed to be Grandma

started to laugh really hard at something a girl with short hair said. They leaned together and looked over their shoulders.

"Are they laughing at us?"

"I can only imagine," Grandpa said, but he was smiling, as if he got the joke.

I think my dad was in high school when Grandma died. I don't even know what she died of. It's not something that I think about very much, because I never knew her. But when the long-haired girl pursed her lips, I could see the way that my father pursed his lips, and the way Julia pursed hers. I don't know why, but the connection between what was real from my own life and these strange, old, dead people, and not knowing where I was, or whether I was really alive—it made me feel dizzy, like you do when you get to the top of a tall building and you look down.

"Let me get this straight," I tried again. "You're dead? And when you're dead, you get to go back to college?"

"It's not just college. It's all my life. I go from memory to memory, and I don't know how long I'll stay or which one I'm going to land at next. It's an unpleasant flashing. Just as I'm starting to understand what I'm seeing, I'm whisked to someplace else. Now, with you, for the first time, I'm able to stop and really look. To breathe. To talk to someone."

I didn't quite know what to say to that. It was nice he was enjoying this, but what I wanted to know was how, if we were stopped inside his memory, was I ever going to get back?

"I'm guessing this is the first day of chemistry class," Grandpa went on. "It was September, and Stella and I were in the same lab. She asked me to tutor her. I was good at chemistry but too stupid to understand that she didn't actually need my help. It took me more than a year to get up the courage to kiss her. I guess, actually, I never did—she was the one who kissed me. I was so dumb."

I'd never kissed anybody, or even come close. Gus has, but only at camp. "But you got married," I said. "It must have all worked out in the end." The girls were starting to gather up their books to go inside, and in spite of my worrying about being able to get out of this memory, I found myself wanting to know what happened next. "Are we going to get to see you soon?" I asked. "It must be amazing to watch yourself."

"Oh, no, it's horrible," said Grandpa. "All these memories are horrible. All I notice are the mistakes, what I did wrong. How I didn't say what I meant to, how scared and shy and angry I was. I hate seeing all the opportunity wasted." A soldier walked past us, toward the wooden classroom door. He reminded me a little of Ewan, the way Ewan looks down at the ground and not up at the faces of the people around him. But mostly the soldier looked like my dad, except that he wasn't as tall. What was similar was the way he stepped lightly, as if he was afraid of making too much noise.

"That's me," Grandpa said.

"Yeah," I answered. "I guess I knew."

"You notice that way of walking?" Grandpa said. "It came from growing up in an apartment, living with too many relatives. There was never enough of anything. Everyone was always telling me to be quiet."

"Dad does it too," I said. "He stoops a little."

"Does he?"

"Hey, I can't even tell what color your hair was, it's cut so short," I said.

Grandpa made a face. "I don't understand why I was so embarrassed about my hair all my life," he said. "It was curly, beautiful, just like yours."

I put my hand on my head. "I hate my hair."

"Really?"

"It makes me look like Ronald McDonald. And my dad hates it too. He's always trying to make me cut it. My mom just says it makes me look cute, which is kind of worse." Then I told Grandpa what I'd never admitted to anyone else. *Who's he going to tell?* I thought. *He's dead.* "But if I cut it, I'll look even shorter."

Grandpa burst out laughing.

"Do you think it makes me look taller?"

"Does it make you feel taller?"

My face went hot.

"You keep it just the way it is," he said.

"Thanks." I wondered what it would have been like to have him be my grandpa when he was alive. I had this idea that I could tell him things, and he'd be the one coming to watch my basketball games, and he wouldn't care if my team won or if I played. Under his plaid shirt, his shoulders sagged, and I wondered if he'd been thinking the same thing. I tried to touch him, but I got so cold I pulled my hand back like I'd touched fire. "Are you—are you *really* dead?" I asked.

He cleared his throat, a phlegm gargle. "Yes," he said. "I'm dead. Though I feel good. I have no idea what's happening, but I feel good. The first time I saw you, you were in your room, with your dad. Daniel. That first time I felt you, there was something electric between us. I've been wondering what made it happen. You have your grandmother's eyes—I'm wondering if that's why we have a connection. But maybe it was something else. What were you talking about with your dad?"

"You," I said. "Sort of."

"Your father was talking about me?"

"No," I said. "I was wondering why no one was acting like it was a big deal that you were dead."

Grandpa winced.

"Sorry," I said. "I guess I shouldn't have told you that."

"It's okay," said Grandpa, though he didn't exactly look like it was okay.

"It felt like a shot when it happened," I said. "Like I was getting a shot. It hurt."

"I didn't know that," he said, and he looked momentarily sad. "But the energy! I felt myself wanting things. I felt myself having the strength to want things. The spinach. Speaking out to your father. And to that other boy, your friend."

"He's not really my friend," I said.

"Well, whoever he is. When you were with him, I felt a little bit like I could help him." He looked tired again. "Was it horrible, coming into the river? You were crying."

"The what?" I said.

"Oh, sorry," Grandpa said. "I don't know why, but the only way I can explain this place I'm stuck in is by calling it a river. It's a cold river, with strong currents."

"I thought you said you were inside your memories."

"Yes," he said, "I am—but the memories are inside the river. They're strung together in long tunnels that I travel through without knowing where I'm going next or why."

"I thought I was dying," I said. "Before."

"Are you comfortable now? You're not afraid?"

"A little," I said. "But I don't know. There's something about your voice that makes me feel all right."

"Ah, Michael," he said. "That's important to me to hear you say. Thank you for saying that. Now, look!" he said. "Look at what a coward I was."

In front of us, the young version of Grandpa stopped at the end of the lockers, looking over at the girls as if he wanted to join them. "Are you watching?" Grandpa whispered.

"Yes," I whispered back.

The young version of Grandpa took a step closer to the girls. The one with long hair—Grandma—turned around and caught his eye. "Watch her smile," Grandpa said. "It's the brightest smile you'll ever see."

Sure enough, Grandma gave Grandpa a smile that made her whole face change. She looked like the kind of girl who would build forts out of bedsheets and let you eat ice cream when she babysat.

The young version of Grandpa stared at her a second, then looked down at his shoes, and turned away, scowling. "Coward,

coward," the Ghost Grandpa muttered. "I thought my memory of it was worse than it actually was, but I see now I was as cowardly then as I remained always."

"You're not so bad," I said, thinking, *What's the big deal? He's just shy.*

But already, he'd said, "Let's go." He put his hands on my shoulders, and it wasn't a gesture of reassurance, the way some-times people will touch each other without thinking about it. He was clearly grabbing on to me for a reason. He closed his grip, closed his eyes, braced himself, and said, "Hold on."

"But I thought you said you couldn't control it," I said. "I thought you said you went through the memories without knowing where you were going to end up."

"Except with you," he said. "There's something about our combined energy that lets me choose a little bit. It's like being in a boat in a storm. You get tossed wherever the storm wants you to go, unless you have a motor and can push the boat against the storm. I don't know where we're going now, but I do know I want to get away. You will help me do that. There's something about the connection we have. Together we make a motor."

Where his hands were touching me, I started to grow cold—I imagined his hand leaving a frozen print on my skin, like a burn. I didn't want to be his motor. I wanted to be warm.

"No," I said. "Don't do this to me. I'm not ready." But I heard the rushing wind again, and the cold intensified, spreading through my body. I tried to draw away, but he wouldn't let me go. When I twisted around, I caught a glimpse of Grandpa's face. His eyes were closed, and he had a fierce look to his mouth, like he was trying to open a jar. "Let go of me!" I shouted. "Stop." But he didn't let go.

The river of the dead felt like water, but as I said before, water that was so cold it was about to freeze—it felt thicker, almost like a jelly. It was heavy on my body, and I felt kind of like I was drowning, like the cold jelly-water was being pushed down my throat.

And then, over the wind, I heard a sound like someone sobbing. Someone *was* sobbing. I could swear it was me—it felt like it was coming from inside my head. It took me a minute to realize that I must have been inside one of the memories Grandpa told me he traveled through.

I was a little boy sitting on a twin bed, holding one of those gliders made out of wood thinner than a Popsicle stick. It was broken. A grown-up voice said, "That will teach you to be more careful."

Just as I felt how miserable that little boy was—I felt his disappointment as if he were me—the space I was inside started to move. I pushed down through the mattress, tunneling away from the boy with his dark red shoes, watching him fade above me.

I stopped in a dark movie theater, leaning forward in my seat, my stomach twisted into knots of laughter. The laughing was hurting me. I could hear the music of the kind of stupid cartoon that's on TV at six in the morning. It was black and white, and it was loud—too loud. I thought it might explode my head. What was so funny? I wanted to know, but I was rushing, moving through the memory, tunneling through the back of the theater seats.

On the way, I saw the red leather shoes laid out on newspaper—I remembered staring at them. The toes were creased, and the soles were worn. I remembered how much I hated to polish them, how I was told to do it every single night.

With my next push forward, I was leaning against a woman's leg, and I knew that it was my mother's leg, except it wasn't my own mother, it was a much bigger leg, inside a dress, and there was a hand pushing at my head. "Move along, Saulie," she said. Saul was my grandpa's name. "Can't you see that Mommy's counting?" And sure enough, there she was at the kitchen table with piles of pennies and nickels laid out before her, and she was scratching notes on a column of newspaper. This time, I pushed right through the kitchen cabinets, and even though it should have hurt, the only pain came from the bitter cold and pressure all around me.

I saw Stella. I was looking at her face. And I loved her—her eyes blinking, her freckles, the bend in her nose I knew so well, the places I knew how they felt under my hands. One of her eyes grew larger, grew and grew until it was a lake, and I was standing at the side of it, watching my own dad dive off a float into the water, except I wasn't thinking, *There goes my dad*, I was thinking, *There goes my son*. And I hadn't known he could make a jack-knife, and I was proud of him.

I spun in the dark. I remembered what Grandpa had said

about a boat in a storm. The cold burning in my shoulders spread down my arms and into my hands. I closed my eyes and felt the tears that were pushed out of them freeze into bullets of ice.

Every point where bones connected in my body ached. And then the cold slowly began to recede, and in a few minutes, I felt first my toes, then my fingers, and finally my face begin to warm. I was lying on the floor of our foyer, just as if I'd fainted. I opened my eyes when I heard the elevator beeping. I saw my mother stepping out into the apartment. I hadn't been that happy to see my mom since—I don't know—kindergarten.

"Michael?" she said. "What are you doing lying in here on the floor? You look horrible."

For a second, I thought I would see Grandpa next to me, or at least back in the mirror. But he wasn't there.

I stood. My knees were wobbly. My head was spinning. I felt like I'd just gotten off a roller coaster, the kind that is really old and made of wood, and probably ought to be shut down. I stuck a stiff arm out to brace myself on the mail table.

"I'm fine," I said to my mom. "I was just resting." Though in fact, it was a few minutes before I could really move, I was still so numb with cold. Fortunately my mom's cell phone rang, and it was a client—by the time she was off the call, and back to find out what was going on with me, I was playing video games on the couch and looking like nothing was wrong.

Chapter 6

After school, Gus came by to give me the homework. I was lying in bed, reading the book we'd been slogging through in English, *Great Expectations*. Up until then, I'd been hating *Great Expectations*. I'd been stuck on page ten for a week. But now I was turning page after page, laughing out loud at some of the funny parts. Was it me reading? Or was *Great Expectations* like spinach—something Grandpa was enjoying through me? I didn't know. The big news as far as I was concerned was that I was warm. Grandpa and the cold feeling that came with him were completely gone. It was a coincidence that *Great Expectations* had started to get easier to read. Or maybe I was still in shock.

"You're reading?" Gus said, tossing the list of assignments on my knees. "You must really be sick."

"If I tell you something, will you promise not to tell anyone on the basketball team, especially Trip?"

"Okay," Gus said.

I took a deep breath. Before Gus came by, I'd decided I wouldn't tell him. What if he told Trip Hall, and suddenly Trip was coming up behind me in school, saying, "I see dead people" in some really creepy voice?

But now that I was alone with Gus, all I wanted to do was have him be my friend, have him be the one I would tell something like this right away.

I put the book down on the floor and sat up. "This is going to sound strange," I warned him. "But something happened to me. Something connected to my grandfather who I told you about this morning, the one who died."

"The one you didn't know?" Gus shook back his straight black hair and narrowed his eyes.

"I sort of did know him," I said. "Just not since I was seven." How did I tell him the next part? "Okay," I started. "I think Grandpa came back to life inside me today."

I felt so stupid during Gus's silence. "I saw him in the mirror," I went on, as if details were going to help. "Standing where I should be. It took me a long time to figure it out. But he was my reflection. And remember when I was yelling at my dad this morning?"

"Yeah?"

"That wasn't me talking, that was him."

"Oh, I get it," Gus said. "This is a game."

"No, it's not," I insisted. Though I realized as soon as he said it that this sounded like the kind of game we used to play— pretend for a day you were blind and walk around with your eyes closed. Or try to get all the way through a meal speaking only in Pig Latin.

"You know how Ewan lives with his mom? Well, his parents

57

aren't divorced. His dad's dead, and my grandpa passed me a message for Ewan from his dead father during assembly today." Did this make sense?

"Is Ewan's dad really dead?" Gus said. "Or is that part of the game?"

"It's not a game," I said again.

Gus was knocking Julia's old American Girl doll Felicity off the chair she was tied to in the prisoner of war camp. "You saved this?" he said.

"It was your idea," I said.

"Look, Michael," Gus said, turning from the dolls to me. It sounded like he was about to explain something big, except he stopped talking.

And just then, for that exact moment, I was tired of pretending. "Do you believe me?" I asked him, point-blank, and I think we both knew that I was asking him more than that. I was asking him if he still wanted to be my friend.

"I don't know," he said. His answer sat there between us, making me feel a little sick, even though I was already thinking that it was my fault, maybe there was something I could do to change his mind.

"I don't even get you anymore," he went on. He looked around the room, as if he'd left something of his in my exploding dresser drawers, or on the half-taken-apart prisoner of war camp. I thought about saying, "Do you realize 'get' is one of the most overused words in the English language?" Three months ago, he would have laughed.

But now he didn't look like he would. "I've got to go."

"No," I said, and I don't know what made me so brave. "Either you're my friend or you're not. And if you're not, then you should say it."

"Michael, don't make it like that."

"You're making it like that. You only want to hang out with me outside school."

"That's not true. I don't know. Why do you have to make this a big deal? Why can't you just let it go?"

"Then you're not my friend," I said. "Go home."

For a second I thought he was as lost as I felt. Then he drew his lips into a line, and he turned around and he left.

I sat on my bed, stunned. I had never believed he would go. Here's what I was thinking: *If I were taller . . . If I were good at basketball . . . If I were funny . . .*

I remembered Grandpa as a little boy sitting on his bed. A little boy who had to polish the shoes that were so worn my mom would have put them in the trash, a little boy who cried over his broken airplane.

I jumped up and stood in front of the mirror a long time, staring into my own eyes. "Come on," I said aloud to the mirror. "You're real, aren't you?" But Grandpa wasn't there.

· · ·

What happened next was so strange I forgot all about Gus and Grandpa. At least for a little while.

It started with a smell. A good smell. Coming from the kitchen. When I went to investigate, I saw that my mom was standing over the stove, stirring something inside a pot. When I got closer, it looked like spaghetti sauce. Laid out on the counter were packages of chicken breasts.

"What's going on here?" I said.

"What do you mean, 'What's going on'?" she said. "I'm cooking."

"What's the occasion?"

"What kind of an occasion do you need there to be for your mother to cook dinner?" This was my mom being funny. She caught a glimpse of herself in the microwave. "I hate this gray."

I opened the pantry. "Don't you dare snack," she said. I withdrew my hand from a bag of chips. I heard the elevator beeping and I ran out to the hall to tell Julia about Mom's cooking. I found myself face-to-face with Dad instead.

I know this is kind of a weird thing to say, but he looked a little embarrassed to see me. Maybe because I have so much personal experience with being embarrassed, I know the signs. He didn't look me in the eye. He didn't put his briefcase on the hall table at an exact right angle to the mail tray, the way he usually does. He didn't put it down at all. It was as if my body were surrounded by a force field—he couldn't come all the way into the apartment because he'd have to pass by me.

Or maybe it wasn't so much that he looked embarrassed as that he looked different. His hair was perfectly combed and polished looking as always, but he must have forgotten his second shave, the one he does at the office. The stubble on his chin and jaw made his cheeks seem hollow. His shirt was wrinkled, his tie was loosened, and he was carrying his suit jacket instead of wearing it. "Are you okay?" I said. "Why are you home?"

He was able to walk past me now. He laid his briefcase on the table and spoke with his back to me, as he took his cell phone out of his pocket and plugged it into the charger. "It's so strange I should be with my family at dinnertime?" he said.

"Yes," I wanted to answer. "Yes, it really is."

Instead I ran back into the kitchen to find Mom. "Is there something I'm missing?" I asked. "Dad's home. You're cooking. Is it Thanksgiving?"

"Dad called and told me he was canceling a meeting and were we free for dinner? So I bought groceries on my way home."

"But we're always free," I said. "And that's never made him want to have dinner with us before."

"How about you set the table," Mom said in her that's-enough tone.

When Julia came home from ballet and saw my dad in the dining room pouring water into glasses, she ran up to him, threw her arms around his neck, and shouted, "Daddy!" I guess that was more the reaction he'd been looking for, because he kissed her on top of her head. "Hello, princess."

Casually, as if it were no big deal, she asked him, "How come you're home?"

And he answered her just as easily, "You know I always want to be home with you guys, don't you?"

I don't know how I know this, but I do: he was lying, and it made me so mad that I wanted to shout, "You don't. You're a fake." But instead I said, "Can we watch TV while we eat?" and my dad gave me a look and said, "You don't expect me to dignify that with an answer, do you?" This was my family in a nutshell: Julia gets "Hello, princess," I get, "You don't expect me to dignify that with an answer."

Twenty minutes later, there we were, all four of us sitting down at the table my mom had to pull out from the wall. With place mats. With knives, forks, and even spoons, which I'd originally left off because who ever uses spoons to eat dinner? Mom made me add them in.

It was like we were trapped inside an ad for Chef Boyardee. Dad said, "This is delicious." Julia "mm'd" her agreement. Mom smiled at them and reminded me not to hold my fork like a pencil.

I had had about enough. "How come we stopped going to see Grandpa?" I asked. I might as well have set off a stink bomb under the table. My mom put down her knife. My dad looked over at her and said, "See?" Julia glared at me, like she was an honorary grown-up and her special grown-up job was to keep me in line.

"What?" I said to all three of them, though I guess I knew what. "Can't I ask a simple question?"

"Michael—," my mom started, but my dad cut her off.

"It's okay," he said, enunciating carefully, which is what he does when he's mad. "I've been meaning to talk to you about this since you asked me about it this morning."

"Fake, fake, fake," I wanted to say, because I hadn't asked him about it. I'd told him.

"Your grandfather did everything he could not to have to see or talk to or have anything to do with other people. He chopped his own wood and lived on groceries he brought into the cabin once a month. He had no friends, except the occasional army buddy who still sent Christmas cards and would make the mistake of traveling through Vermont and looking your grandfather up. And he didn't want to have a family. When we came to visit him, it was like pulling teeth to get him to step out of his routine—he did the same chores, the same meals without thinking about what we were eating and when. He didn't want us there, and I didn't want to be there."

Dad picked up his fork, as if he was going to show how not upset he was by taking a bite of Mom's actually-pretty-tasty chicken Parmesan. But he couldn't do it, and he put the fork down.

"He didn't want you to come?" I said. "He actually said that?"

My mom cleared her throat. "He wasn't a bad man," she started, but my father cut her off again.

"He wasn't a man at all." My dad was talking faster now, though he was still pretending to be calm. "A man takes care of his family. A man is there for his children. A man welcomes grandchildren. Your grandfather—" Now Dad was looking at me and Julia, and I knew this would drive her crazy, that she was getting in trouble for something I had done. "Just be glad that you have a father who loves you. I come home for dinner. I am a part of your life."

"But—," I started. I was going to point out that this was the first time Dad had been home for dinner since I could remember.

And the Grandpa I had met wasn't like Dad was saying. But I knew no one would understand. This may sound stupid, but Dad acted like everything I did was wrong, and Grandpa acted like everything I did was a miracle. He loved me. That is, if he was real. He *was* real; I knew he had to be because he'd been so nice to me. Nicer than Dad, who only ever wants to correct me and tell me what to do.

"Fork, Michael," he said now.

See?

. . .

"Michael, come here a second," Julia called through the bathroom when she heard me brushing my teeth later that night. I stepped into her room to find her sitting at the long white table where she IMs her exchange student friends and stays up until midnight doing homework because she gets in so late from ballet.

Last year, Julia redecorated her room by ripping up the pink carpet, taking the posts off her canopy bed, and painting everything white. There's nothing out on the shelves or bureaus except two big pictures of Mom and Dad, her jewelry box, and the glass dog collection from when she was little.

"Um, shoes?" she said, and I shrugged off the sneakers I was still wearing.

"What's with the obsession with Grandpa?" she asked.

"It's not an obsession," I said.

"I'm not criticizing you, Michael," she said. "I'm just surprised. It's kind of, I don't know, mature."

"I guess I'm the only one in the family who thinks it's weird that someone dies and we don't even do anything about it."

"I should also point out," she said, "that you are totally dense. Why do you think Dad came home early for dinner? And Mom cooked? Dad's sad and wants to be with his family, but he didn't want to make a big deal about it, and then you go and make it sound like he was this horrible person, not visiting Grandpa."

"Sometimes I want to smash one of your glass dogs with my fist," I said.

"I'm sick of those dogs anyway." Julia looked down at her big fat precalculus book, then up at the computer screen. She always wins. "But why Grandpa?" she went on. "I bet you can't even name all of the cousins on Mom's side. And you didn't care about Grandpa any more than you care about them."

"Maybe I know Grandpa better than those cousins," I said.

"Were you in touch with him?" she said. "Did you write him a letter or something, before he died?"

"Not exactly."

"What do you mean, not exactly?" she asked. But I just turned around and left her to stare.

Chapter 7

In school on Friday, I passed the daily quiz on *Great Expectations*. I guess when you do the reading, that's what happens.

In history, we were talking about the Depression, and I told the class how my grandpa lived at home and went to City College while he was in the army. Ms. Gellert was like, "City College wasn't founded until the end of the Depression. And aren't you a little young to have a grandfather that old?"

"Oh, yeah," I said. "I guess he did say it was the fifties."

"But it's nice to hear from you, Michael. Family context is what brings history alive."

Whatever.

Fourth period, we had art. I used to look forward to art because art and earth science are the only classes Gus and I have together. But today I was dreading it for the same reason. After what he'd said the night before, would he not talk to me at all? I hated the idea of that so much, I decided I wasn't going to talk to him.

I got there late, so I wouldn't have to deal with Gus. But I guess he had the same idea, because he got there even later. So we ended up next to each other, in the last two seats, at the same table as Ewan.

I didn't want to look at either Ewan or Gus, so I buried my head in my book bag, pretending to look for some gum.

We were learning how to silkscreen T-shirts. All the girls were making flowers on their shirts, and all the boys were making comic book characters. I was making the Hulk.

Ms. Rosoff had told us to try something simple, and that abstract worked very well, but I thought the Hulk looked easy. I hadn't realized that the lines that look so simple when you see them on the page get very complicated when you try to make them yourself. I'd kind of imagined feeling bigger because of him on my shirt, and feeling protected from other people laughing at me. But my Hulk was coming out looking like a giant green blob. I couldn't tell his arm from his head.

Gus was making the Japanese flag, a red circle in the middle of a white T-shirt. Gus lived in Tokyo for a year with his mom, who is a financial expert on Japan and speaks the language fluently. In their house they eat a lot of sushi, and always have Pocky sticks and Japanese comic books, which Gus pretends he can read. It used to kind of confuse me, since Gus's mom is Indian, but the one time I asked her why she wasn't a financial expert on India, she rolled her eyes and said, "You sound like my mother."

Ewan's face was screwed up in concentration, his shoulders lifted up around his ears as he filled in his design, which was the road, of course. I knew I should say something to make him feel better about his dad, but I couldn't think of a thing that would be helpful.

Gus finally broke the silence, which I think surprised Ewan as much as it did me. "I heard about your dad, Ewan," he said. "I'm sorry." Ewan looked up, but he didn't say anything. Eventually, he just nodded, and we all buried our heads back in our work. So what, I thought, it doesn't matter if Gus knew how to do the right thing with Ewan. He didn't do the right thing with me.

Ms. Rosoff circulated. She stopped by our table, looking over Gus's shoulder first. "That is stunning, Gus, really exceptional."

At Ewan's T-shirt, she sighed, and said, "I ordered extra gray. It should be in by tomorrow."

I tried to block mine with an arm so that she wouldn't see it too, but she leaned over my shoulder anyway. She usually says something fake and encouraging to me like, "I love your use of color," but today she ignored what I was working on entirely. "I need to see you in my office after class," she said.

Stepping over to the sink area, Ms. Rosoff clapped her hands. "Cleanup time, everyone." Her voice would have sounded like a kindergarten teacher's if it hadn't been low and gravelly and weak from the cigarettes. Everyone filed out of the room except Ewan, who asked if he could work a little longer on his project. Gus didn't even look at me as he walked out the door.

Ms. Rosoff's office is supposed to be a supply closet, but since it has a tiny window, she's shoved in a desk and a couple of chairs and made it extra-claustrophobic by covering the walls with students' artwork that she likes enough to save if they don't collect it at the end of the term.

I saw a picture Gus had drawn in September. It was of his own reflection in the mirror of his bathroom. He'd made his face look all angles and sharp lines. And there were three of Julia's photographs. She'd done a series of ballet dancers' feet; Ms. Rosoff sent them in to a city competition and they won a prize.

But I didn't have much time to look at the art, for Ms. Rosoff had squeezed herself into her desk chair and beckoned for me to sit across from her in the straight-back chair jammed behind the door. She was wearing something so much worse than her usual big purple dress—gold pants, black sweater, gold dangling earrings, and gold socks with black bows on the ankles. She looked like a bumblebee.

"Michael," she said, turning to me, her gold pants crinkling. She was wedged so far back into the chair she had to wiggle her body from side to side in order to lean forward. "I want to talk to you about your gift."

No art teacher in the world has ever told me I had a gift. "My what?" I said weakly.

Ms. Rosoff gathered herself like a black and gold bird puffing out its feathers. "I'm talking about what you said yesterday," she said. "To Ewan. About his father. The one who spoke to you from the beyond."

"What?" I said.

"You were telling the truth, weren't you, when you said you didn't know his father was dead before you spoke to Ewan?"

"Yes," I said.

"I didn't understand what I was hearing immediately," Ms. Rosoff said. "You've always struck me as someone with low creativity, and it's unusual for a gift like yours to take hold so strong in someone so little."

"I'm not little," I answered.

"I meant your age," she said. "Twelve is very young."

"I'm thirteen."

The correction didn't faze her. "Even so," she went on. "You must have very open parents. Sometimes, the children of seers—" I think at this point she realized that I wasn't following her. "Do you know what I'm talking about?"

"No," I said.

"What happened to you yesterday in assembly hasn't happened to you before?" Her voice was coy, like the answer just had to be yes.

"No," I said.

"Michael." I think she was finally starting to understand that I was completely lost. She opened the narrow window above her desk, turned on a miniature fan, and lit a cigarette. I didn't mention that we were in a smoke-free zone.

She took a long drag, closing her eyes. She blew out a smoky breath of air. "Throughout the course of human history," she said, "certain people have been endowed with the ability to communicate with those who have gone before."

"Do you mean dead people?"

"Well, yes," she said, nodding solemnly. "But they're no longer people, exactly. They've turned into something else. I don't know if you're aware that there has been a great deal of reporting on the ways that the dead communicate with the living. Every civilization that has left any kind of written record behind makes reference to it. Always, there are select people who are sensitive to communication from spirits who have lost their physical form. These special people are called seers. Some seers hear rapping, some are elevated into a trance, some call spirits to show themselves through the levitation of objects. When I worked as a handwriting profiler and analyst, this subject was of great interest to me."

"Are you—" I couldn't remember the word she had used.

"A seer?" She looked at me straight in the eye as if what she was about to say was going to take me completely by surprise. "I am not." She drew in a breath and held it, like she was trying to keep herself from crying. "I have not been chosen for this," she said. "I think that you have."

The laugh started as a cough, a pocket of air stuck inside my nose, a reaction to the cigarette smoke. It ended up coming out my nose and mouth at the same time, sort of a cross between a snort and a brain explosion.

Ms. Rosoff ignored my laugh, turning her back for a second, as if giving me a chance to take off my clothes in privacy. She dropped the cigarette butt in a little bag she kept in her purse.

"Years ago," she said, "my mother died, and even after we cleaned out her apartment—the one I live in now—I could not find a special ring that she had always promised would be mine. I went to a seer I knew from my work as a handwriting analyst, who told me to look under a phone book in the back of a closet, and I

found the ring exactly where she said it would be, inside an envelope with a note that said it was for me. My mother had dementia
at the end of her life, and must have left it there and forgot where
it was. I can't tell you how much it meant to me, to know that she
was thinking of me, that her spirit is still in the world, and that
she cared enough to send the message."

Ms. Rosoff turned back to face me. Her eyes had filled with
tears, and suddenly, I felt sorry for her, with her purple muumuus
and her dead fish eyes. I know it's not the same, but once, when I
was little, I got lost in FAO Schwarz. I didn't panic but went to
the glass elevator, sure that as I rode up and down in it I would see
my mom. Which I did, only I hadn't realized that once I saw her
I wouldn't be able to get her attention. There she was looking for
me behind the stuffed animal displays, talking to the security
guards, and I was inside the elevator, banging on the glass, but she
couldn't hear. I didn't get scared until I saw how scared my mom
looked, pointing the guards in one direction after another,
squeezing the sides of her head between her palms. Is that what it
felt like, to be dead, to be watching the living? Or to be alive
when someone you knew really well was dead?

"Michael," Ms. Rosoff said, "tell me about your gift."

"Um," I said, feeling like I'd been asked a question about
homework I hadn't done. First of all, I didn't have a gift. Grandpa
was the one in control. And second of all, I really didn't like
being this close to a strange grown-up in such a small room.

"It was my grandpa," I said, mostly because I couldn't think
of a lie, but as I started talking, it felt good to tell Ms. Rosoff what

had been happening. I could tell that she believed me. "He died, and yesterday, I saw his memories," I went on. "He spoke using my body. I saw things about other people, things that only someone who was dead could know about."

"Yes," Ms. Rosoff said. "That's called channeling. The spirit of a person who once lived comes into your head and controls you from the inside. They're often in communication with others who have passed into the spirit world."

"He made me eat spinach," I said.

"Yes," said Ms. Rosoff again, as if my eating spinach was the most exciting thing she'd heard in years. I glanced down at the black bows on her gold socks. Maybe it was. "Tell me more."

"He came and took me last night to where he went to college, and it was really, really cold inside the river of the dead."

"What?" she said, for the first time sounding surprised.

I repeated myself. "The river of the dead. That's what he called it. You know, he could make tunnels through it, but it was really cold."

Ms. Rosoff squinted, took my chin with her thumb, and moved her face close to mine. "Michael, now you're beginning to tell a story." She let my face go.

"It's true," I said. "Honest."

"Look," she said, "there's no need to exaggerate. This is how so many seers get in trouble—trying to pretend they can do more than they can. But no matter. I can help you. If you want to talk about your gift, see my friend Charlisse. I can take you, but I also will give you her card. Because if you want to live up to the kind of story you just invented, you will need to train." She handed me a piece of thick, cream-colored paper the size of a playing card.

Charlisse Hillel-Broughton
768 Park Avenue, Apt. 8A
New York, NY 10021
212.555.1737

"I wasn't lying," I said.

She closed my hand around the stiff card and nodded for me to go. "Charlisse can help you."

. . .

I ran all the way down the stairs to the first floor, where the lunchroom is. I didn't even glance over to the loudest table in the room, where the basketball guys were cracking jokes, and Gus was laughing with Trip. Somehow, I made it through the line, emerging with a peanut butter and jelly sandwich.

I was too busy thinking about all the things Ms. Rosoff had said to care that I looked like a loser, sitting with Ewan for the third time in two days. Maybe I was a loser. Even the craziest woman in the world, who believed in psychic channeling, thought I was telling lies. At least Ewan, who was reading a book with a picture of a kid's body twisting around planet earth, wouldn't make me talk to him. And now that I knew about his dad dying, I guess I understood why he always looked like he'd just been slapped. With my own dad, I could imagine him stopping an oncoming car with his open hand, kind of like Superman, before I could imagine him being dead.

I'd never thought about it much, but suddenly the fact that Dad—anyone—can go from being alive to being dead—it gave me a chill. And then I started thinking about how stupid I was to take PB+J on a Tater Tot day.

Just as I was thinking of asking Ewan if he wanted to trade his, he put his book down, slapped both of his hands on the table, and said, "You weren't lying. I know you didn't make any of it up."

"What?" I said.

"I was listening. From the art room. Ms. Rosoff doesn't know what she's talking about." I must have still looked blank. "You told her about going with your grandfather into the river of the dead."

"You heard that?" I said, feeling panic rise. "Did anyone else?" I had a vision of what Trip Hall would say if he found out some teacher-lady thought I had seen a ghost.

"I knew it," Ewan said. "I knew you'd gotten a message from my dad. But you weren't just channeling through your grandfather. You were doing a lot more than that. People try to make channeling simple, but it's not."

"She told me I was a seer."

"You're not a seer. Something else is happening to you. It's rare. And dangerous too."

I felt scared by what he was saying, but also a little proud of myself. "How do you know?" I asked. "How do you know any of this?"

"Because I read," Ewan said. "All I do is read. And all I read about are ghosts."

Chapter 8

Half an hour later, Ewan and I were sitting in the living room of his mother's apartment. It looked the way you'd expect the dad's apartment to look, if the parents are divorced. A half-eaten muffin had left a trail of crumbs to a cup of coffee on the low table in front of the sofa. Piles of magazines sometimes topped off by books lying on their faces to mark a place covered the rest of the surface area. I noticed a pair of socks, and a wineglass with a bead of dried-up red wine at its bottom. Ewan's mother's shoes were heaped under a small table by the window. A door behind the couch led to Ewan's bedroom, which was just big enough for a bed and a desk, which in turn was just big enough for a gigantic computer. The computer was covered with magazines and books, just like the coffee table in the living room. There was no TV.

"Where does your mom sleep?" I said, and instantly wished I hadn't asked the question, because his face went red. "Here," he said, and I realized that the couch pulled out. His mom didn't even have her own room. "It must be nice, not having any annoying older sisters around," I said, hoping that would make up for hurting his feelings.

"I cut classes all the time," he announced.

"Really?"

"I started doing it about a month ago. I guess because I'm new, no one remembers if I'm there or not."

He could see that I didn't believe him. "Think back to the last class you had with me," he said.

"Art, duh," I said.

"Okay, before that."

"History."

"Right, history. How do you know I was there?"

"I don't know. You probably said something, got called on, gave an answer—I don't know."

"I wasn't there."

"You weren't?"

"I was home," he said. "Sitting right here, eating that muffin, and starting this book, which I'm about to finish."

"Doesn't your mom find out? Won't she catch you?"

"She's working," he said.

"When does she come home?"

"Late," said Ewan. "When I don't have work study, a babysitter comes to pick me up at school at dismissal, and she makes dinner for me. So I have to be sure to get back there by three."

I thought of the space in our apartment—the living room where Julia runs through her ballet routines next to the shining black piano, the foyer where Mom puts up a Christmas tree every year even though we're technically Jewish. We have so much space, and Ewan has just enough room to read in. His mom doesn't even have a place to put her shoes.

"So," Ewan said, adopting a businesslike tone. "Your grandfather. You must have been very close to him."

"No," I said, and I explained how I hardly knew my grandfather, how we stopped visiting.

"Do you have any of his stuff?" Ewan asked.

"Like what?"

"Something he gave you—his watch, or a handkerchief, anything that was close to him, anything that might even have smelled like him."

"I wouldn't *want* anything that smelled like him."

Gus and I would have laughed at that, but Ewan acted like he didn't even know I was joking. "So you don't have any of his stuff."

"No," I said.

"That's unusual," said Ewan. "A ghost needs something to connect to. Something that he loved, or even just knew very well. That's why people always see ghosts in houses where the dead person lived. Or sometimes, when people are murdered, they have a strong connection to the place where they were killed."

"How do you know this stuff?"

"Books," he said. "I told you."

"But aren't they made up?"

"Kind of," Ewan admitted. "But I think they're based on stories that get told and retold, and that have some relation to things that actually happened at some point. They all end up being the same story over and over."

"Is it because of your dad?" I said, feeling stupid for even asking, because duh, why else would he be doing this? What I was really wondering was something different. "Have you—you know—" I knew Ewan believed in this stuff, but even so, I felt like he was going to think I was an idiot. "Have you seen your dad? Since he died?"

Ewan was biting his nails. "No," he said and put his hands in his lap, as if he'd just noticed he didn't have any nails left to bite. "Well, sort of. I've had a couple of dreams. I guess you only get to see the dead if you're really lucky. There has to be something about you. An openness. I thought I might have had it. The dreams are kind of like that. It's like, he's in my room, or with me at school, and I'm showing him around, and . . ."

"And what?"

"And when I wake up, I don't feel sad. I feel like I've actually *seen* him. It's like, when we lived in New Hampshire, sometimes he would pick me up at school. When I came out of the front doors, I'd see him, leaning on his car, waiting, and that's what the dreams are like. I wake up with the feeling that he's waiting for me, if only I could catch up."

"Wow," I said, because everything else I could think of—like, "That's so sad"—would have come out sounding sarcastic.

"Don't worry about it," said Ewan quickly. "I'm fine." And then he changed the subject so fast, I knew just how weird it was for him to talk about his dad even that little. "Your grandfather," he said. "Do you think he could have been murdered? Didn't you say he and your dad didn't get along?"

"My dad didn't murder him," I said.

He started to bite his fingernails again. "I just don't get it," he whispered to himself. "How did your grandfather connect?"

I remembered something Grandpa had said. "I have my grandmother's eyes," I said. "That's what he told me, that I have her eyes, and that they were familiar to him." I thought of something else. "I first started to feel him after my dad and I were fighting." I didn't tell Ewan that I'd told my dad I didn't think he cared that Grandpa was dead. It wasn't something I wanted anyone else to know. "And he said that he has to push through tunnels of his memories, that that's what it's like to be dead, but that when I was there, he got to talk to me, and he could start breathing, which feels good. He looked really bad when I first saw him, but by the end he looked better."

"Better?"

"Like, healthier. You know, his skin was pinker."

"Oh my God," said Ewan. "This is huge."

"When he wanted to get away from what we were looking at, he put his hands on my shoulders. I got really cold, but it sent us back into a tunnel, and that time I saw some of the memories we were pushing through. I think."

"Wow," said Ewan. He held still for a minute, forgetting his fingernail. "That is so cool."

Ewan's being impressed made me feel like a big fake. I remembered how certain Gus had been that I was making it up. "No," I said. "It's stupid. It can't be real. I mean, really real. Isn't it more possible that I might have made it up? You know, hallucinated."

Ewan was staring at me, his eyes squinted in confusion. "Hey," I said, "I'm just trying to be honest. A lot of people would never believe something like this."

"Do you even know *anything* about ghosts?" Ewan was using the it's-unbelievable-how-stupid-you-are voice he often slips into when giving the answers in class.

"No," I admitted. "Except that I don't really believe in them."

"Look," Ewan said. He stepped into his room, and came out with an armful of books. *Ghostly Encounters, Surfing the Third Dimension, The Surreal Planet, Dr. Occult.* He stepped in again and brought out another armful, and kept at it until a new layer of books was covering the tiny coffee table, and half the couch was littered with books as well.

"I've read all of these," he said. "And I've been online. I've looked at every Web site I can find."

I was starting to feel the way I did the month before, when Ewan and I had to write an oral report together about Brazil. Before we'd even had our research period, he collected all these notes on NAFTA (which is some kind of government thing that my dad couldn't believe I'd never heard of). Ewan told me how NAFTA affected Brazilian people who couldn't get money from the government to buy cisterns for collecting water. "Isn't all the stuff about them in Spanish?" I'd said. "In Brazil," Ewan had answered slowly, as if I were deaf or really, really stupid, "they speak Portuguese."

Now he put a hand on the tallest pile of books and said, "Let me tell you something about ghosts, Michael. They come back for a reason." His voice was cracking with excitement, which is totally embarrassing. Or should have been—Ewan didn't seem to notice. "They only have the power to do things they really, really want to do. They don't waste time. You'd think they would— they have forever—but they tend to be very focused on getting a particular thing, or reaching a particular person."

"They are?" I said.

"Of course," he went on. "There is a barrier between us and the other dimension, and it takes a lot of energy to pass through it. Everyone thinks of ghosts as wispy, smoky things that can walk through doors, but really, to them, their bodies are solid. Imagine what it would take for you to break through a brick wall."

"I couldn't do that," I said.

"Well, you probably could, if you knew karate, and could focus your energy in the right way. And that's like a ghost. They can only get through the wall if they build up enough energy and force to break something that seems totally impossible for them to break through. Although sometimes they don't even know what it is they're looking for."

"But I don't even feel him anymore. He's not with me."

"Yes, he is," said Ewan. "Here, take my hand."

"No way," I said.

"Do you have to be so conventional?" he said.

I gave him my hand.

"Now hold on to me while I try to pull away."

I held on, and he started to twist his hand and move his wrist. "Do you feel that?"

"Yes," I said.

His hand stopped moving. He kept it still.

"Do you notice that as much?"

"No," I said. "I mean, I can tell I'm holding your hand."

"What you felt with your grandfather at first was a struggle. He was struggling to connect with you. But now he's not struggling anymore. The connection's wide-open. That's why you don't feel it."

I was starting to feel too warm, like maybe it was time to get out of that tiny, overheated apartment.

Ewan looked at his watch, which was black, big enough to be a calculator, and strapped to his wrist with red mountain-climbing rope. "We've got to get back," he said, and I didn't protest.

· · ·

As soon as Ewan and I hit the cold air on the sidewalk outside his mom's apartment, Ewan took a swig off his inhaler and started to run. I followed, my backpack bouncing against my body. By the time we got to the corner market where kids from Selden buy Pop Rocks, soda, and gum, my chest was burning from breathing in cold air, and my hair was sticking to my face. I felt better.

"Do you really think he's coming back?" I said as we stood catching our breath.

"They always do," Ewan wheezed. "What happened to you, I think it's something called slipping. You talked about the river.

83

Well, I think you're slipping into the river of the dead. While you're in there, the ghost is harnessing your living energy. It's your body's energy—combined with his very strong desire for something—that gives you the power to tunnel through the river. That's why he looks better. He's breathing through your body. And it's why he needs to be touching you to take you back out. I think when you look at him in the mirror, when your eyes are touching, that gives you the energy you need to go in."

"That's cool," I said.

"Slipping is very cool, but it is also extremely dangerous."

"Dangerous how? Grandpa's already dead."

"It's dangerous for you. Once you've made a strong connection to a ghost, it's like driving in a car with no brakes. You can push the accelerator, but you can't stop—he'll just keep sucking and sucking until there is nothing left. Or at least, I think that's what happens. There aren't very many people who have slipped who remain alive long enough to report on it."

"Remain alive?" I repeated. "As opposed to what?"

Ewan grabbed my elbow. "Don't worry about that now. I'll call my babysitter and tell her to meet me at home later, so I can spend some time in the library. I'll try to find out more, but in the meantime, you have to remember this. You cannot look in mirrors, or at any kind of surface that might have a reflection. That's all it could take, any reflective surface—" He stopped.

"And what?"

"You could slip again. And this time, you might not be able to come back."

Chapter 9

Ewan's last words were, "Act normal." It was easier than I
thought it was going to be. As soon as I was back inside Selden's
carved oak door, school was just school. The stairs going down to
the gym smelled like disinfectant and Gatorade and echoed with
the sound of sneakers squeaking on the wooden floor.

When I opened the gym door, there was my team—the
eighth-grade team—but there were too many bodies, and with a
sickening feeling, I remembered: there was some kind of coaches'
meeting downtown, and varsity, JV, and the eighth-grade team
were practicing together.

It didn't take me long to find Gus—the only eighth grader on
varsity—shooting a layup, his ball hanging in the net for one perfect second. "Ugh," I said out loud, and headed for the locker
room, where I stared into the mirrors over the sinks, willing my
eyes to turn into Grandpa's.

Ewan had said not to do this, but I had to see—was
Grandpa really there? It had been almost twenty-four hours
since I'd last seen him, and as convincing as Ewan had been
about the danger, I thought it was more likely Gus was right

about all of this than that Ewan was. Gus was usually right about everything.

And anyway, I wasn't afraid of mirrors. I wasn't afraid of Grandpa. I was afraid of dropping the ball in front of Gus and all his basketball friends. I was afraid that I'd say "Sorry" every time I missed a shot or threw a pass over someone's head.

"Get me out of here," I said to the mirror. Nothing happened. "Grandpa?" I tried. "Please?" Nothing. Eventually, I had no choice but to step out into the cold of the gym.

Gus was running laps, and he jogged past me. He didn't say hello, and I just stood there, watching his shorts swish back and forth—his special varsity shorts that brushed the tops of his knees. Because of my size, I still wear lower-school shorts, which are cut much higher than the new uniform. I hiked them down as far as they could go.

Mr. Ball blew his whistle the second I stepped into the gym. "Okay," he shouted. "Bring it in." We all jogged toward him, and he leaned against the wall with his clipboard.

"Today is all about threes," he said. He blew the whistle three times in a row for emphasis. Mr. Ball is a big fan of the whistle. "Three-on-three half court, okay?" he said. "Playing to—?"

"Three," the eighth graders groaned, but the kids from varsity and JV didn't know what he was talking about.

"Winner stays on the court," Mr. Ball went on. "Loser rotates out. At the end of practice, the top—how many?"

"Three," the eighth graders mumbled.

"I can't hear you."

"Three!"

"That's right. The top three players get to sit on the bench while everyone else runs sprints. How many?"

"Three." Now the older kids were groaning along in answer too.

"How many sets?"

"Three."

"And that would be suicide sprints," he said. "Oh, and by the way, all *three* players must touch the ball once before a shot goes off, or it doesn't count. That's *three* passes minimum." He held up three fingers, as if even after his mentioning it three hundred times in the last three minutes, we might not understand what the number three meant.

It's hard to make fun of a coach whose name does all the work for you. Once, last year, Gus asked him, totally straight-faced, "Do you think it was *destiny*, that your last name is Ball and your job is coaching sports?" Gus paused right after the word "destiny," as if he were taking a moment of silence to honor some amazing spiritual force. For a long time, I couldn't think about the way Gus had leaned on the word "destiny" without cracking up. I glanced over to where Gus was standing with Trip now. He was looking at Trip, who was holding the ball out in front of his chest.

"One?" Trip said, push passing the ball to Gus. "Two," Gus answered. Trip was scanning the room for one of his buddies, PJ or Russ, to be their third, and I started to wonder if there was anyone else on the eighth-grade team I could play with, but just then the gym door opened and everyone turned to see who was there. Was someone late? Sometimes Mr. Ball made us run sprints when someone was late, like we were in a let's-turn-these-bad-kids-on-the-basketball-team-around movies.

But it wasn't a kid. It was a dad. My dad.

Other parents come to school all the time, especially to games and practices. Mr. Green, the headmaster, is always running down from his office to tousle kids' hair in front of their parents, as if that's what he does all day. But my dad rarely comes to anything. "You can't come to the games and also pay for the games," he says. "I have to be at work."

So now, seeing him, my first thought was that something was wrong at home and he had come to get me. Our apartment had burned down. Or maybe Mom was in the hospital. But he only nodded a hello to me, made his way over to the bleachers, climbed up, and sat leaning forward with his elbows on his knees.

I wondered—how did he know how to look so much like the perfect dad who comes to all his kid's games? Was it TV?

"Your *dad's* here," Gus said. I guess in his shock he'd forgotten he'd decided not to be friends with me anymore. "I know," I said, and in the next second, the ball Gus had been spinning between his palms was coming toward me. I had enough time to lift a hand in front of my chest for protection, swatting at the ball and bending back my pinkie finger at the same time.

"Ow," I said, holding my finger. I looked up at my dad. He was wincing.

Gus said, "Michael, you're our three."

"No," I started to say, but Trip beat me to it.

"No way," he said.

"Sorry, I already called it," said Gus.

"But I want to win." Trip was almost whining.

"He's playing," Gus said, and I was a little surprised at how much he could stand up to Trip. "Look," Gus said. "His dad's here."

"You don't have to be nice," I said, but Gus was already pulling a red scrimmage vest over my head. I looked over at my dad. He hadn't moved. The whole thing made me feel like I was going to throw up. First of all, I hated how phony it felt. Gus was acting like my friend, but he wasn't my friend. He was making me feel like a charity case. Second of all, what Gus was trying wasn't going to work. Playing with Gus and Trip was only going to make me look like a jerk in front of my dad. And third . . . Well, this is hard to explain, but I also hated how nice it felt too, to have my best friend sort of back, even though it was only because he felt sorry for me. I hated how nice it felt to have my very own dad in the bleachers—his shiny black hair, his tallness. I hated feeling nice, because I knew I was only going to end up feeling disappointed.

We were first to play—up against Trip's friends PJ and Russ, and the best kid from eighth grade, Steven Kline. Trip and PJ checked the ball in, and Trip dribbled into the back of the court. Russ stood in front of me, poaching so that he and PJ could double-team Gus. Trip looked from Gus to me. I held out my hands for the ball, not because I wanted it, but because I knew you were supposed to look like you did.

"Get in there, Michael!" I heard. I hardly recognized my dad's voice shouting out like that. I wondered if it felt weird to him too. I had to concentrate, I told myself, because Trip looked like he was about to pass to me. But then he didn't. He sent the ball to Gus, who managed to catch it even though he was being double-teamed.

"You weren't really open, Quasi," Trip said quickly. "You were being poached on the basket side. And your eyes were closed." While I was trying to figure out what he was even talking about, PJ started waving his arms up above his head to keep Gus from making a shot. Gus took a dribble to the left and one to the right. He finally shot the ball in my direction, just past PJ's left hand.

"Please, please, please," I prayed. "Don't shut your eyes." And I didn't. I kept them focused right on the ball, the orange leathery rind, the black stripes. Without thinking too hard, I put out my hands, and then I felt my fingers gripping the outside of the ball in the same way Gus's and Trip's did. Easily.

When I looked up, my dad was pressing buttons on his cell phone, checking messages. I knew he was e-mailing the office, or whatever. I'm sure if I asked him, he'd point out what a huge sacrifice it was for him to even be there. But couldn't he have been watching? Catching that ball was, like, the highlight of my season.

I looked back to the court. I knew what Mr. Ball would be shouting if we were in a game. *Just get rid of it*, I told myself.

But I didn't get rid of it. I looked from left to right, and suddenly, I realized that with PJ and Russ double-teaming Gus, no one was covering me, and I was open to take a shot.

I took a second to make sure I was holding the ball the way I was supposed to, my fingertips lined up under the seams. I jumped, trying to spin the ball by pushing with my arm and flicking my fingers. Just as I knew that the most important thing in the world was getting that ball through the hoop, I was sure it wasn't going to go in. But then it did go in. It went in with a swish.

I tried not to act like it was a big deal, but I felt as good as if the perfect swish had happened in my own body. It was like someone had thrown open a window in a musty room, and fresh air was blowing in. I was taller, I could feel it. I felt my shoulders lifting back and my chest rising.

I could hear my dad clapping. "Yeah, Michael!" he called out. I looked up at him, and he was looking at me, just looking, and it was really cool because I could tell I was being the kid he wanted. But it was also not cool. That basket was a fluke. I never made shots. I never even took shots. He wouldn't have to watch much longer before he saw me fumble.

The next time we had the ball, Trip passed it to me. To my continuing shock, I caught it. I passed it off to Gus, who ran in for a layup.

"Go, Michael, yeah!" my dad shouted.

"One more," Trip said. Then, to me: "Just because you don't totally suck doesn't mean that we have this in the bag. Focus."

But it was Trip who lost his focus. Next time he had the ball,

PJ d-blocked him. "Come on," Trip said, groaning at himself in the way I'd thought he'd be groaning at me.

PJ dribbled into the back of the key, and Trip lunged for the ball, knocking it out of PJ's hands, then chasing it down and smacking it with one hand so it bounced high into a dribble. "Kimmel," he said, and I was surprised he even knew my last name. He faked a pass to me, before sending the ball hard over to Gus, who was ready, and sent it right back to me. Again, I held the ball high up over my head, got my fingers underneath it, and watched it swish right into the basket.

"That's three!" said Trip, and he actually high-fived me. "Way to go, Quasimodo," he said.

"Maybe you can call him Quasi-good-at-basketball-o," said Gus, and Trip laughed, as if all along the nickname had been a joke.

Gus, Trip, and I held on to the court for three more games while my dad watched, his cell phone gripped between his hands like he was holding a pole on the subway. I never saw him check his messages again the rest of the time he was there. He was calling out in the same way as Trip, who seemed to see not just the ball but also the players moving inside his mind, the way I saw them on the screen when I was playing NBA Street. He was yelling to us when there were holes to fill and telling us when there were opportunities to pass.

After the fourth game, when Trip, Gus, and I were drinking water, my dad came over and patted me on the shoulder. "I've got to leave now—I've got to get back for a meeting."

"Are you coming home for dinner again?" I meant it to sound like it wasn't a big deal either way, but it came out pathetic.

"We'll see," my dad said. "We'll see."

"Wait, Dad," I called after he'd already turned his back to go. I don't know if I really wanted an answer to the question lurking in the back of my mind, or if I was just trying to come up with a way to make him stay a few minutes longer. "Do you know if Grandpa was any good at basketball?"

"Grandpa?" he said. I wondered if he was going to give me another lecture about how Grandpa didn't love anyone, as he had the night before.

"He did play basketball," my dad said. No lecture. "He played varsity at Roosevelt High School in the Bronx, and I think his team won some sort of championship the year he was captain. Maybe they were all-state?"

"Oh," I said. My dad was giving me a look—like, why are you interested?—and I tried to make my face a blank.

"Michael," my dad started. He seemed like he was going to say something, thought better of it, and then said it anyway. "You're the one who is good at basketball now. I'm impressed."

I almost said, "Don't get used to it. I think it's Grandpa playing, not me," but I didn't. Suddenly I wished I'd never seen Grandpa, never found out that he died, never talked to Ewan, never played basketball with Gus and Trip while my dad looked on. It felt unfair. Unfair to who? Or as my dad would say, unfair to whom? I guess it felt unfair that we had this perfect family all of a sudden, and Grandpa was left out in the cold. Or maybe "unfair" wasn't the right word. I don't know if this makes any sense, but it was like something on the back of a comic book. "Miracle family! Just add water!" Way too good to be true.

The thing about winning a lot of games is that you have to keep playing. Our water break was over. Trip, Gus, and I were tied with PJ, Russ, and Steven's team for first place. The game to decide the winner has about to begin.

I started off with the ball and checked it in with Steven. He was so much taller than me, he had to look down to shoot it back to my chest. I passed it off to Trip, who faked into the basket, then ran to the back of the court. Gus was already running from the top of the key toward the basket, and Trip sent the ball bouncing hard in front of him. Gus scooped it up while using his shoulder to block PJ from making a defensive grab. Before anyone knew what was happening, Gus had taken a layup shot and the ball was hanging in the net, swinging slightly from side to side before dropping through.

Gus dribbled the ball to the top of the key. He passed it around the key to me, and I passed it back to him. Trip ran in under the basket and Gus shot the ball in so Trip could get a layup. He outran Russ to the ball, and got it in.

Trip pointed at Gus. "One," he said. He pointed at his own chest. "Two." He pointed at me. "Three?"

I nodded. It was my turn to score. I was starting to believe that I could actually do this.

But that was before I ran into the key to grab a pass from Trip, and felt a twinge in my leg—I must have twisted my knee. It was just enough pain that I couldn't move to the left when Steven rushed at me. He swiped the ball out of my hand, getting off a quick shot to PJ, who shot to Russ, who shot back to Steven, who beat me into the key, shot, and scored.

With my next step after Steven's basket, the twinge in my knee turned into searing pain. I stopped running and grabbed my thigh. Now it wasn't just my knee that hurt, but my head, and strangely, my heart. It was beating so fast that it felt like it was throbbing. What was this? Why did I suddenly feel as scared as if the lights had gone out and a hand had grabbed my throat? I wondered for a second if other people could tell.

Woven into the pain so that I didn't know if it came from my knee or my head, there was blood. Salty, bitter, and also kind of sweet. I could smell it and even taste it on the back of my tongue, as if I'd swallowed some. Behind the blood, I smelled mud and grass and body odor, kind of like a soccer game in the rain.

And then, with no warning, I felt myself pushing into a memory, one of Grandpa's. I wasn't with Grandpa. I wasn't slipping. I was in the middle of the gym. I was at school.

But no doubt about it, I was also inside a place I'd never been before. This time the slip came like something you see in a flash of lightning, and then it was gone. But it still felt as real to me as the pulsing pain in my knee, which seemed to worsen with every passing second.

I saw a field of trampled long grass streaked with mud and ripped apart by craters left by what I knew were falling enemy shells. This was a war. The sky was a burning, brilliant blue, and hanging in it, frozen in motion, were hundreds of clumps of dirt raised into the air by a shell that had just landed. I saw dark red patches on the ground. They were bodies. Men. Some held hands up to protect their faces from the dirt and shrapnel falling from the air. Some were rolled into tight balls, and others lay twisted in ways that made me think they were dead, or at least broken. One man was half buried already, his face covered but for one eye.

"Get in there, Kimmel," Trip was shouting. I looked to Gus. I felt like I was going to pass out.

"Are you all right?" Gus asked, and all I could come up with was, "My knee just started hurting."

"Do you need to stop?"

"No!" I said, and Gus gave me a look because I had shouted. "No," I said, more calmly, because I kind of thought that if I stopped, the memory was going to come back.

It came back anyway. There was another flash and I had to squeeze my eyes closed against the pain. I was back on the pock-marked field, but this time I wasn't looking at the memory like it was a photograph, like before. This time I was inside it. The dirt that had been frozen in the air was pouring down like hail, and I felt something strike my knee. I was moving—on the ground, my face pressed up against a clump of grass, trying to push my body off the field. I was gasping for air. I saw the torn-up earth, pieces of shells, discarded canteens, packs, packed-down grass, a cloud of chaos. And then I managed to get my body to move forward. With each push, I felt my knee burn, and my insides heave.

How could this be happening? I opened my eyes again and saw the gym. I was back, right? So how come I was also slipping? I had no idea what was going on.

"Is this an injury?" Trip was asking, looking from Gus to me. I was standing on my good leg, and to someone watching me, it might have looked like I had squeezed my eyes closed to keep the sweat from stinging my eyes.

Yes! I thought. *I'm injured.* All I wanted was for someone to come get me and carry me to the bleachers so I could rest. But if I rested, would I slip further in? Ewan had said, "Act normal." At this point, I wasn't really sure I knew what that meant. "No," I spat out, answering Trip. "It's not an injury."

"Okay." He shrugged. Gus opened his mouth as if to say something, but when I glared at him, he closed it again. PJ passed Steven the ball, which Steven caught easily since I was supposed to be defending him. Steven passed it off to Russ, who took a jump shot from the outside, and scored again. "It's two-two!" Trip shouted. "Let's get it back."

I tried not to think. About my knee, about the twisted bodies, about the feeling of gasping for air with dirt falling onto me like snow. The taste of blood was still on my tongue.

With PJ dribbling at the key, Trip poached off Russ, so that he could cover Steven. I said, "I've got him."

"You don't," Trip growled, and he was right because I could barely move with the pain in my knee. Trip ran back to Russ just in time for Steven to pass Russ the ball. Trip raised his arms to his sides, shutting down every option Russ had to pass it. Finally, Trip swatted the ball away from him, in Gus's direction. Gus picked it up and passed it off to me. I can't believe I caught it—my hands and even my arms were trembling.

"Was that three passes?" Trip shouted.

"Just two," Steven grunted back at him. So I passed off to Gus, who passed it quickly to Trip, who ran in to take the layup, and missed. I was right there, under the net, and I jumped up for the rebound. I was one step in front of Steven, and I knew I could get it.

That was when the bad knee twisted under me. The pain was like two pieces of metal rubbing together, and it sent me right back into the war. In this memory, I was taking a break from crawling across the battlefield to the medic tent, and my face was right next to a shiny piece of a metal—a canteen? In the metal's reflection, I was watching something, and what I saw made my stomach contract.

It was the Selden gym. It was there, for just a second, and when I looked away and back, it was gone. And then it was there again—the yellow floorboards, the honey-colored bleachers, the boys in their jerseys, and in the front of the memory, me—my hair soaked with sweat, my face flushed, holding the ball, which I'd just caught. It was like time had stopped and then twisted back on itself. Before, when I had been looking in the mirror, I'd seen Grandpa. Now Grandpa was looking in a mirror, and he saw me.

Somehow, seeing the gym, seeing the boys, gave me strength. It was like a picture of home, or the face of a good friend cheering me on. I felt Grandpa lift himself onto his forearms and start to move forward again.

"Keep going," I muttered, inside the memory. Was it me talking to Grandpa, or Grandpa talking to the boy in the gym? "The trick is not to feel," I said. "You cannot feel the pain. Just keep going."

And then I opened my eyes, and the war was gone. I was back inside the gym. PJ was rushing toward me with his arms up, and I started waving the ball in the air, as if I was going to throw it. I was trying to show Grandpa that I was still in the game. It might not make any sense, but I thought I was rescuing him by doing this.

But with my next step toward the basket, I fell, letting the ball roll out of my hands. PJ scooped it up. Trip started covering him, and Gus took on Steven and Russ all by himself, his arms extended, moving side to side. I half raised myself from the floor.

"Are you playing?" Trip said.

I nodded my head, because I couldn't talk. I stood up, putting all my weight on the good leg. PJ was coming in for a shot, and I knew without having time to really think it through that I could block the shot only if I jumped onto the bad leg. Which I did, slapping the ball in Gus's direction.

I had never known anything worse than that pain. It felt like a needle the size of a pencil boring into my knee. I choked on something. Had I bitten my tongue?

Gus grabbed the ball and lobbed a shot over Steven's head to Trip, who ran in for a layup to win the game. I was up now, and limping. I knew I had to get away. I was heading for the locker room. Gus ran to join me. Mr. Ball was asking if I was okay, and I was saying, "I just need to pee."

"What's wrong with you?" Gus whispered.

"I've got to get out of here," I said. "Help me."

"Where do you want to go?" he asked. For that minute at least, it didn't matter whether Gus was my best friend, or sort of my friend, or not my friend at all.

"Here," I breathed, pushing open the locker room door.

"What are you doing?" Gus laughed nervously. "What's going on? Is it a sprain?"

My hands were clenched into fists. "I want to look in the mirror," I said.

"Huh?" said Gus, but I was already standing in front of the sinks. And then I was looking at the glass.

The habit of seeing your own self is so strong that in the first instant of seeing another person in your reflection, it doesn't register. Then, there Grandpa was, his eyes wide with pain, like mine, his own fists clenched. His forehead was red and blotchy and he looked like he was about to cry. "I'm getting us out of here," I said, and the reflection said the same thing right along with me.

The cold came on faster this time. I didn't feel it spread, it just hit me like I'd walked into a wall of water. I heard the rushing sound of the river, and felt my feet slipping as the ground was replaced by cold all around. My heart shrank under the pressure. I couldn't breathe.

I entered a memory. I was watching Stella again. She was unwrapping a cheese and margarine sandwich. We were sitting on the red vinyl seats of an old-fashioned train. I was hungry, and she was talking, telling a story about the bread. The train passed through a meadow, and as I remembered the meadow where the battle had taken place, I moved inside a new memory, as if my body had traveled through the window of the train. It was the day before the battle, and the grasses we would destroy stood tall. I was with another soldier and he said, "It's hard to believe such a beautiful place is so dangerous." I nodded my head, thinking, *Don't say things like that aloud. If you're soft, you'll die.*

I slipped into another memory. I was leaning in a doorway watching a teenage boy work on math from a book lying open on his desk. The boy—my own dad, but in the memory he was my son—did not look up or act like he noticed I was there. I wanted to speak to him. I wanted him to notice me and look up. But "How's the homework going?" or "What are you working on?"—it sounded trumped up. It sounded too little. And too late.

I floated up now, up, up into the cold of the river. My feet were kicking behind me as I almost swam. The rushing was deafening, and I felt the cold cracking in my elbows and my poor, sore knee.

Chapter 10

When the cold inside my bones and the sound of rushing wind began to recede, I heard Grandpa's now-familiar voice. "You're here, Buckaroo." It was him—his voice—that was making me warm up. The heat started inside my body, behind my ears, and was working down to my rib cage, up my neck, down my legs, and into my arms. My fingertips and nose were still numb with cold.

To my great relief, Grandpa wasn't young anymore. He wasn't in the war. He was back to the same cut-short white hair, the same wool shirt. We were safe.

I sat up and took a look around. We were on the porch of a house. I followed Grandpa's gaze out beyond the porch and saw a lawn stretching about a hundred yards or so down to a lake that was dotted with sailboats and a few white-capped waves. I could just barely see across the water to a far shore that was nothing but a thin blue line. "Where are we?" I asked. "What is this?"

"You mean the lake?" he said. I did mean the lake, but I also meant all of it—his being dead, my being able to talk to him, to feel him, to see inside his memories.

"My friend Ewan says that what's happening to me is called slipping."

"That's a good word for it," said Grandpa. "As I told you before, I don't really understand any more than you do. I only know that when you are with me, I can breathe again. I feel warm. I smell lemon meringue pie."

"I hate the cold parts," I said. "And some of the memories—" I didn't know how to describe them. "Some of the memories hurt."

Grandpa's face lost a little of the pink glow it had taken on, and I felt bad. But he had to know. "They hurt me too," he said.

"But you're a grown-up. They're your memories," I said. "I'm a kid. Aren't you supposed to protect me from the really bad stuff?"

"Yes," he said, and he sounded sad. "But I don't seem to be able to. I'm not sure protecting you is the way to keep you safe."

That didn't make any sense, so I moved on to another question. "When I was inside your memory of the battle, I saw my own self in the gym at my school. I was reflected in that canteen. Was that what you saw when you were in the war for real?"

"Yes," he said.

"You saw me playing basketball? For real? Me?"

"Yes," Grandpa said. "I didn't know who you were until now. I've always thought that was a hallucination."

"Weird," I said.

"Indeed," Grandpa answered. "I'd have said impossible. But now a great deal more feels possible than I used to believe."

"I have one more question," I said. I was kind of embarrassed to ask it, but I did anyway. "My dad said you played basketball. Was that me playing in the gym just now? Or were you playing through my body, the way you made me eat spinach?"

"What made you think it was me?"

"Well, I could catch. And shoot. And get open when I needed to be."

"It's fun, isn't it? Basketball. God, I loved it."

"It was fun this time. Usually I hate it. I feel like people are watching me and I can't do anything right."

"Hmm," said Grandpa. "I never felt like anyone was watching—I'm pretty sure no one ever was. I loved the concentration it took to play well. I loved how it could make me forget everything else. I would see only the ball, and the other players."

"Oh," I said. I remembered how cool it had felt when Grandpa told me he'd had really curly, crazy hair like mine. I'd felt like, wow, someone really understands me. This wasn't another moment like that. "I guess it was you, then. I guess I'll just go back to being bad."

"I don't know if it was me. I saw you play, but I don't know if I was playing. I don't know how any of this works. But think about oatmeal right now. Think about spinach."

"They both sound kind of good."

"I think you'll like them now. For the rest of your life. And I think you'll be able to play basketball now too. Don't ask whether it was you on the court or if it was me. There is no me. There is only you. Whatever part of me that's inside you is yours to keep.

104

"We're connected now, Michael," he went on. "I thought I had control of it, but I don't. You pulled me in today. When you felt that pain, the energy of your response brought me to you. I don't quite know the extent of it, but it seems that this connection is more flexible than I'd thought."

I wasn't really listening to him. I could feel myself smiling. That was me on the court! I could play basketball.

"Wow," I said. I hadn't realized how much I'd even wanted to be good at basketball. I'd been so busy hating basketball that I hadn't paid attention to how fun it is when you can actually play. "Wow," I said again. I felt like the happy feeling was expanding now, outside my body, into the floorboards of the porch, out into the air.

"Hey," I said aloud. "Is this *the* lake?" I looked behind me. "Is this your cabin? Your cabin that you lived in in Vermont where we would visit you?"

"The very same," Grandpa said.

"But it looks so different," I said. "There were woods here, where this grass is. You couldn't see the lake at all from the cabin. It looked farther away."

"It did," said Grandpa.

"It's nicer this way."

Grandpa narrowed his eyes just a bit.

"Sorry," I added.

"No, you're right," he said. "The way it looked when you used to visit me is very different from how it looked when I first came here. When Stella—your grandmother—was alive, everything was different."

"How did she die?" I asked him.

"She had cancer." He paused as if he was going to leave it at that, then thought better of it and kept talking. "She lost weight one summer, but we didn't think too much about it. And then she went to the doctor, and four months later she was gone."

"That's terrible," I said.

"It was very hard on your dad. She loved him, and he loved her. When she died, he was left alone with me, and we didn't know each other. And I didn't want to be alone with him. I wanted Stella back. Stella had been the glue between us. I think he was marking time from when she died to when he could go away to school. He finished high school early."

"And you came up here."

"Yes, just as soon as he went to school, I sold our house and moved up here for good." He sighed, and I started to put my own memories of Grandpa's cabin together with the place we were seeing now. It was strange to think that the lawn I was looking at would be so grown up with trees that by the time I was a little kid, I would think of it as the woods. We'd never sat on the porch when we'd visited—Grandpa used it to store the huge amounts of firewood he split from trees he chopped down by himself. But the porch was actually really nice, perched up high above the water.

"The woods are what happens if you don't take care of a lawn," said Grandpa. "After Stella, I stopped mowing. It turned into a meadow, and then it turned into brush, and after a few decades, it was woods."

"This is what it looked like the other day," I said, thinking about the memory I'd had of my dad diving off the dock. "Was that when you were remembering it?"

"Oh, yes," said Grandpa, sighing. "I was thinking about your dad. I was thinking about how proud I was of him for learning that dive. Or how proud I am, seeing him this time. Back then—I don't know what I felt. Fear, I guess. I lived in fear."

"What were you afraid of? That he'd drown?"

"No," Grandpa said. "Nothing like that. I was afraid I'd drown. Drown in feeling."

"I don't understand."

"I don't either," he said. "But that summer . . ." He paused. "That summer your father spent days and days in the water. There were kids up and down the shore, New Yorkers mostly, people who rented, people who came every year. He was a part of it, and I was not. I wish—" He stopped again, and waved a hand, as if to say, "Forget it."

"What?" I pressed. He looked so sad, I wanted to help him feel better.

"During the summers Stella and your dad spent here, I was working hard in the city. I came up on the weekends, but many times I would call at the last minute to say I had to work. The truth was, the work wasn't always urgent. My problem was I didn't know how to be up here. Stella and your dad, they got up in the mornings, got dressed in their bathing suits, went to the water. They dove in, and then your dad splashed around while Stella made breakfast, took care of the cabin, and gardened. There was nothing for me here. I didn't want to slow down enough to actually absorb any of it. I didn't like to swim. My favorite summer up here, I painted the whole cabin. When I sat still, I felt so . . ." He had to take a minute to find the right word. "Lonely."

I didn't know what to say.

"But there's nothing to do about it now," Grandpa added. "So come on, let's go for a swim!" His voice strained with the effort of changing the subject, but he ran down to the water and jumped in, drawing his knees to his chest to make a cannonball. He broke the surface with a splash, and the water rose in giant sparkling drops. Grandpa ducked his head under. He started to tread water. He waved, but I didn't wave back because my mouth was hanging open.

Grandpa's hair wasn't wet. He was still wearing all his clothes. I walked closer to see more, and noticed that water was beading up on his shirtsleeves.

To see what would happen, I dove in too, and found that the water felt warm and soft, and yet it was not like regular swimming because I wasn't getting wet and neither were my clothes.

"Is this what it's like?" I asked, treading water next to Grandpa.

"Is this what what's like?" Grandpa was looking at me with wide eyes, as if he had no idea what I could possibly mean. Suddenly, I was embarrassed, as if I was going to tell Grandpa something he wouldn't want to hear, like his fly was down. But I was too curious not to finish the question. "Is this what it's like being a ghost?" I said.

"Oh, that." He sounded so sad, I knew I'd been right to hesitate before asking the question. "Yes. You want to get wet, to get cold, to feel the touch of another person on your body. That's how it feels when I'm watching you. And when I'm watching myself. I can't change anything. I know so much more, but I'm powerless to fix what I did. It makes me hungry. There's so much I wish was different!

"But you're helping me, Michael," he went on. "With you, I feel stronger. I feel filled up."

"You do?" I said. "But when you were alive, you never sent me presents. You never visited. I didn't even know you before."

"Oh, Michael," he said, and I could see the tears building in his eyes. "I loved you since before you were born. You understand that now, right? Only . . . the fear. It kept me from knowing and feeling love. I was strong—I saved myself in the war, but the strength also froze me. Do you understand how that could happen?"

"Yes," I said, because I did. "Sometimes, with Gus—," I began. But I didn't want to talk about Gus. "Sometimes that's what it's like playing video games. There's this invisible shield around your brain. Nothing else can get in. It makes me feel like nothing can get to me. I like that feeling."

"Don't like it," Grandpa said. "It starts as something you can control. But the problem is, once you grow a shell around your brain—or, you might even say, your heart—it's almost impossible to shed it. After Stella died, living alone in that cabin, my shell grew even thicker. It was all I had. I found myself irritated with other people, even though I was seeing them less and less. I stopped being able to feel anything for other people at all, besides irritation. I wanted to be alone all the time, but even when I was alone, I felt unhappy. I kept thinking I'd feel better if I reduced the sources of my irritation—if I reduced the changes in my routine, interactions with other people, anything that put pressure on me. Do you understand?"

"Yes," I said, because I felt like I almost did, like if I went home and thought about it, it would start to make sense.

"That's my boy," he said, and still in the water, he reached over to give me a bear hug, which of course, I felt only as cold. He pulled away quickly, and I wondered what the touch felt like to him. Was it heat, as he'd told me before?

As if he'd read my mind, he explained. "I don't want to take you back into the tunnels," he said. "If I hold you too long, that's where we'll end up."

I was glad that he'd let go.

· · ·

After swimming, Grandpa and I sat on the porch of the house. We watched a young version of him and my grandmother come through, looking at the dusty insides of the house, and standing on the lawn. "This was the day we bought this place," Grandpa said, as if recognizing an old photograph. "I wonder what brought me to this memory right now. I must have been thinking about all the lost days up here and brought myself to the beginning, to the time when I still had the chance to make it all different."

"Could you have?" I said.

"I don't know," said Grandpa. "I don't know how much choice we have in our lives."

I saw Grandma take the younger Grandpa's hand. She looked the same, but rounder, and she was carrying a really enormous purse. She let go of Grandpa to go to my dad, who looked like he was maybe nine years old. She wouldn't let him get too close to the water, as if she were afraid he could drown just by being next to it.

"She looks different," I said.

"She looks beautiful," Grandpa answered. "They both do."

Seeing my dad as a boy was even stranger than swimming in water that didn't get me wet. His socks were pulled up to his knees—what a dork! When he finally was able to squirm away from Grandma, I followed him up onto the porch, where he started to arrange the rocking chairs into a perfect line, facing out to the water. Then he pressed his face up against the dirty window and peered into the house. I wondered what he was thinking.

The younger version of Grandpa came up behind my dad and tousled his hair. "Thinking of all the fun we'll have up here?" Grandpa said, but he wasn't really looking at my dad when he said it. He was looking at a spot just over his head.

My dad pulled away from Grandpa's hand. "I guess," he said, sounding sullen. "But when will we see you if we come up here? You'll be living at home, and Mommy and I will be up here. I don't want to come up here by ourselves."

Grandpa was watching his younger self intently. I could

almost feel him holding whatever it was he had instead of breath. He flinched as his young version cuffed my dad on the ear, kind of playful, kind of hard.

"Don't be ungrateful," he said. "Do you know how lucky you are to have a lake house like this one?" He rubbed his temple like he had a headache. My dad turned away from him. Next to me, Ghost Grandpa's eyes were full.

"Are you going to cry?" I said.

"Ghosts can't cry," Grandpa said. "It's like we can't get wet. And we can't touch."

"Why weren't you nicer to him?" I said.

"I think I thought I was protecting him."

"Protecting him from what?"

"From his own sadness," Grandpa said. "I didn't want him to be sad. I didn't want him to see that I wasn't a good father. But I wasn't. I wasn't good to him."

I felt so sorry for Grandpa, I forgot for a second about slipping, and I put my hand on his shoulder. I wanted to pat him on the arm, or try to hug him or something—anything. But all I felt was cold.

At first. Then, after I'd held my hand there a minute, there was something else, something warm, a little bit of a tingle.

"Do you feel that?" I whispered, afraid that if I spoke, it would stop.

"No, Michael, don't do that," said Grandpa. "You don't want to have to go in the river yet."

"But do you feel it?" I said. "I can feel you." I had to see what would happen if I left my hand there a second more. I thought I'd still be able to pull it away in time.

"Michael—," Grandpa started again, but I didn't hear what he said next because the rushing sound had returned. The warm tingle of my hand touching his shoulder turned to the sharp bitter cold of the river of the dead, and I saw the red lights spinning, so cold they were hot, the wind pushing tears out of my eyes. "Stop, stop," I begged, trying hard to turn my head against the current of air. Grandpa said he loved me. How could he leave me alone in such painful cold? He was nowhere to be seen.

Chapter 11

As the cold inside the river of the dead froze deeper into my body, I pushed through more of Grandpa's memories. I was sitting in an office, at night, with a deli sandwich, unwrapped and half-eaten, pushed off to the side. In a circle of light made by a small desk lamp, I was checking columns of numbers to make sure they'd been added correctly. I could feel the numbers clicking together like I was stacking dominoes inside a case.

Then I pushed through to another table, lit by a different lamp. I was working a crossword puzzle. I found the "down" words ECHO, ERA, REDUCE, ET, and suddenly I gave a little grimace of a smile to realize that I could connect them all with an "across" word—CLANDESTINE.

I felt safe inside these memories, but also I felt sad, like I'd swallowed a piece of the cold that surrounded me. The tiny bit of light coming from the desk lamps was fading. I squinted at the crossword puzzle, but I could no longer make out the letters.

It was fully dark now, and I switched to a new memory. I was in a movie theater. I was the boy again, the boy who had laughed at the cartoon, but this time the movie was over, I wasn't laughing, all the rest of the people had gone home, and I was waiting for something to return to the screen to take me away from the sad feeling waiting to creep back into my body, where it always seemed ready to come alive.

Then all was light, a blinding, bright sky. I was looking down at the lake from a mountaintop, leaning on a walking stick, gnawing on a piece of salami and sucking cool water out of a canteen. My hips were aching from the hike, but I didn't care. The salami was salty, the wind was pushing clouds across the sky like the sailboats on the water below, and my chest was full of fresh mountain air.

The memories began to speed up, and the cold inside the river of the dead grew tighter, but I didn't let myself pass out. Even though I couldn't breathe with all the pressure on my lungs, I tried to stay awake. At the point where the pressure, and the cold, got so I could feel my eyes rolling back into my head, and everything was growing dark, and noises were distorted as if I'd gone underwater, I cracked open my eyes and saw at the end of a long tunnel of blue light what looked like a miniature drawing of a row of school lockers.

Some of the lockers were open, and one of them had a black sticker with a skull and crossbones on it. I knew these lockers, but I couldn't place them. Then I remembered. They were in the boys' locker room at school. Though they were very far away, I could see them in detail, down to the way the vents on the far left were dented, and the metal was starting to rust.

As soon as my brain understood what I was seeing, the pressure holding me down lifted, and I was catapulted forward. The lockers rushed toward me so fast, I was sure I was going to slam right into them. I put up my hands to protect my face, and then I was lying down on the cold tile floor of the locker room. I felt as though my stomach had been compressed into a walnut. I was shaking from the cold.

I closed my eyes, and the rushing sound receded. I could hear voices.

"All I'm saying"—it was Julia speaking (Julia? In the boys' locker room?)—"is that I'm calling the nurse."

"No, wait," Ewan said, and I didn't know what he was doing there either. "See the color coming into his face? Just let me take his pulse again." I felt his fingers on my wrist. I opened my eyes. Ewan was kneeling next to me. Julia was standing behind him. Her eyebrows were furrowed, and she looked like she'd swallowed something sour. I turned my head to the other side, and there were Gus and Trip, standing. Trip had his head cocked, like a dog listening to a high-pitched whistle. Gus was watching me with the same glaze of concentration he gets on his face when he plays Game Boy.

"He's awake," said Gus.

"Oh, thank God," Julia breathed.

"Are you sure?" Trip asked. He sounded angry.

My lips were dry. "Why are you—all—here?" I managed to get out.

They started speaking at once, then stopped, and Gus pointed to the floor. "After I got you in here, you passed out. Then suddenly Ewan rushes in—"

Ewan interrupted, "As soon as I started researching slipping, Michael, I realized you weren't safe, even at school, even at basketball practice. I came to find you right away."

"I'm not sure what you mean by safe," Trip said. "But everyone was running sprints except us three, so I came in here to find you guys, and Brainiac's making us drag you away from the lockers so no one can see that you're passed out. The whole time you were going crazy." Trip made his body shake and rolled his eyes up in his head. He stuck his tongue out. Was that what I looked like?

"Stop it," said Gus.

Julia turned to me in her I'm-telling-on-somebody voice. "Michael," she said, "Gus and Trip were trying to convince Ewan to go get Coach Ball, or a nurse, or someone, and Ewan wasn't letting them, and I heard this whole conversation through the vent that goes into the girls' locker room. Coach Ball stuck his head in the room to make sure you were okay, and Trip told him you were in the shower. As soon as the rest of the team cleared out, I came in."

"There's a vent?" Trip said. His face was turning red.

"What's important," Julia said, ignoring Trip, "is that I got here in time to see that Michael was having some kind of seizure . . ." She paused to let the word "seizure" sink in, reminding them how serious it was, and how neglectful they had been. Trip and Gus swallowed. Were they afraid of Julia? She continued, "And you were just sitting there watching!"

"We weren't only watching," Ewan said quietly. "I was tracking his pulse. I already explained this. If it went below fifty, I was going to call 911, but otherwise, we'd keep him out of doctors' hands, because they're not going to understand this, or help him. They'd only stick him in the hospital, which is the worst place he could be."

"Michael," said Gus, "that's totally not true. We wouldn't have let you just lie there. We were about to call 911."

"Let me get this straight," Trip said, taking a step closer to Ewan. "A kid's passed out but you say we shouldn't do anything about it because of stuff you read on the Internet? I'm no doctor, but—"

"I didn't find out about the pulse rate on the Web," said Ewan. "I found it talking to a psychic researcher in Australia." He sounded as huffy as Trip. He wasn't taking a step away from him either. "He told me some amazing stuff about slipping, Michael." Then Ewan said to the others, "Michael was traveling in the river of the dead."

"Who are you?" Trip said to Ewan. "Aren't you in my geometry class?"

"He's new," Julia spat, as if "new" was such an ugly word she could hardly bear to say it out loud.

"I don't expect you to understand," said Ewan. "But if you know what's good for Michael, you should stay out of my way."

"Stay out of *your* way?" said Gus. "Michael is my best friend. And"— he pointed at Julia—"this is his sister. And—" He looked at Trip, realizing that Trip was really nothing to me. I guess "tormentor" wouldn't be a very good way to make Gus's case.

"I'm the captain of the basketball team," said Trip.

"Yeah," said Gus, sounding a little less convinced of the point he was making, then revving himself up all over again. "So what gives you the right to tell us anything?"

All three of them were looking at Ewan, and in response, Ewan just looked at me. "Tell them," he said. "And let's just hope they believe you."

"Okay," I said. I was sitting up now. "I know this sounds crazy, and this is what I tried to tell you the other night, Gus, but Ewan is right. He's really smart and he knows a lot about ghosts, and it seems I have one. Grandpa," I said, looking at Julia, who couldn't seem to decide whether to open her mouth or close it. Gus was looking at me straight on, squinting through his hair. Trip was smiling, but in the way people smile when they're finding out there's a KICK ME sign on their back and they're trying to pretend in the first seconds after noticing it that there's a way in which they might have been part of the joke, instead of the butt of it.

"At first it was just little stuff," I explained. "Like I said something that wasn't me talking, or I was eating food that only Grandpa liked. But then I started to see him in mirrors, and when that happened, I started to be able to go into his head. Sort of. I don't really understand it, but it feels like I travel through this tunnel made up of his memories of his life, and then I pop out inside a memory where I can see Grandpa as a ghost and talk to him."

"Only a few cases of what Michael is doing have been recorded," Ewan said. "It's called slipping—he's slipping into a place called the river of the dead. This researcher in Australia said that it's very hard to know anything about slipping because the relationship between the living person and the ghost changes as they spend time together. It's like any relationship—as the connection deepens, the channel that opens up between the two people expands."

"We went swimming together this time," I told Ewan. "But we didn't get wet. Up until now, we weren't able to touch each other—I'd just feel cold where his hand lay on mine. Except last time, I forgot, and tried. There was something there. I could feel him."

"Really?" Ewan said.

"Is that bad?" I asked.

"I think so," he said, his face pinched with worry. "I don't know. This Australian guy said you should try to stop slipping. He said it's not healthy. He said each visit will be more draining than the one before. And going to a doctor is only going to get you locked into a hospital where they'll try to shock you out of what they see as seizures and give you drugs for epilepsy."

"It's not that bad, though," I felt I had to say. "It doesn't hurt when I'm actually with Grandpa."

"The people it's happened to always say that," Ewan said. "It's painful, but they start to *like* it. They start to be able to feel it coming, to control it themselves, sort of. They talk about a willed openness, whatever that means. And pretty soon, they go into one of those seizures like the one you had and they don't come back."

"What do you mean, they don't come back?" I said, but I was glad Trip cut Ewan off before he could answer the question.

"If no one else is going to say this, I will," Trip said. "This is the biggest load I've ever heard." He snorted. "It's crazy. It's like, *Tales from the Crypt* crazy. My dad knows some pretty big-deal Hollywood agents. Maybe he could get you a job writing crackpot movies."

"Your dad's in jail," said Julia.

"It's not a jail," Trip said, speaking low, as if he knew no one was going to believe him, but he had to say it anyway. "It's a detention facility. It looks like an old people's home. There's an apple orchard."

I couldn't help sneaking a look over at Gus. He held his arms crossed in front of his chest, his eyes narrowed.

"Do you believe any of this is real?" I said to Julia.

"Come on," she said. "It sounds crazy." Then she took a deep breath and held it. "But . . ." She let out the air. "I believe that you think it's true. I respect that."

"Really?" I said. Somehow it was harder to imagine that Grandpa had come back from the dead than that Julia respected me.

"What about you?" I said to Gus.

"Honestly, I'm a little scared for you," Gus said. "I definitely thought you were just making it up yesterday, but now I have no idea what's going on."

"Yeah," said Trip. "The seizure didn't look very good."

"Okay," I said, but before I could collect my thoughts, Ewan interrupted.

"Michael, you have to focus," he said. "I don't know how

much time you have. The guy from Australia said he would hop on a plane and fly out here, but that we probably didn't even have enough time for that. He said your best shot was trying to figure out what your grandpa wants, and then helping him find it before it's too late. He said that you'd know what your grandpa wants, that it's probably pretty obvious."

"Um," I said. "I guess I could ask him?"

"You don't know?" As always, Ewan sounded like he was more baffled than angry. Baffled that he could possibly have underestimated my dumbness.

"Just think about it," he said. "Weren't there any clues?"

I put my head in my hands and tried to think for a minute, but mostly what I thought about was the fact that this wasn't going to work. I'm not good at figuring things out. "It isn't fair," I said. I dug my hands into my pockets and looked at Ewan. He was the one who came up with answers, not me. "I've seen so many of his memories, but they don't mean anything to me. I don't know how I'm supposed to understand any of this. This whole thing is crazy. It makes sense that no one believes me. I wouldn't believe me either."

No one said anything for a few minutes. "Maybe we should tell Mom and Dad," Julia finally said with a sigh.

"No—," Ewan started.

"Maybe you are a little bit crazy," said Trip, holding his thumb and forefinger an inch apart. He was trying to be funny, but no one laughed.

"Why are you even here?" Ewan sneered. "None of you

believe Michael." Trip took a step closer to Ewan, and I could see on his face what he was thinking: *the smart kid's gonna get a wedgie.*

"I'm here because," he started hotly, but I think he realized pretty quickly that he didn't know. "Because," he sputtered, "because I'm bored. And Gus is here. And because Michael just played awesome basketball. And . . . and . . ." Now he was starting to sound angry again. "And everyone knows you shouldn't get medical information off the Internet."

"I told you, it wasn't through the Internet like on a chat room or something. I was e-mailing—"

"Can I say something?" interrupted Julia. "I think that we should tell Mom and Dad."

Gus was talking over both of them. "Don't do us any favors, Trip, I mean . . ."

For two seconds I listened to them all fighting. How long was this going to go on? And how was it going to help me?

That's when I felt the raised letters of a business card rubbing against my fingers inside my pocket. Half remembering, I pulled it out.

"Stop it," I said in a quiet voice that managed to get everyone's attention. "Maybe this can help. Ms. Rosoff gave it to me." I showed the card to Ewan. "It's her psychic's card. She told me to talk to her. Maybe she can help."

"Most psychics are phonies," Ewan began, but when he saw the name on the card, he snatched it out of my hand. "Oh my God!" he gasped. "Charlisse Hillel-Broughton. She's famous! You can't get her number anywhere. She only takes on a few clients a year."

"There's such a thing as a real psychic?" said Julia.

"She's as real as you can get," Ewan went on. "Her husband is this British lord or something, and for a long time they lived in India. Now she lives here in New York. I can't believe you have her number."

"And address," said Julia, looking at the card over my shoulder. "Oh my God. She lives in one of those coops some movie stars can't get into. They won't even let you have a mortgage."

"What are you waiting for?" said Ewan, opening my locker and pulling out my clothes. Ewan hadn't lived in New York long enough to care about real estate. "Get dressed."

I looked at Julia, Gus, and Trip. "Will you guys come with us?" I said.

"Yes," said Julia. "I'll give you three hours. But after that I'm telling Mom and Dad."

"You want Trip?" said Gus. And then, more quietly, "You want me?"

My head was still pounding from the cold. "I'm not feeling well," I said. "I can use all the help I can get."

Chapter 12

Julia had money—she always does—and so she paid for us to take a cab. Our cabbie was nice too, and let us get four kids in the backseat, though three is the law. Trip sat with the driver. We pulled up in front of the square white building and stepped onto a red carpet, like we were at the Oscars. Hedges that had been carved into the shapes of roaring lions flanked either side of the polished brass door, which was guarded by a doorman with a trim white mustache, white-gloved hands, and a stiff, unsmiling face. He looked down at Trip, Gus, Ewan, and me without moving anything but his eyes.

Then Julia stepped out of the cab after paying the driver, and you could see the hard corners of the doorman's mouth relaxing. In her perfect, A-student voice she said, "Apartment 13A, please," and when he asked our names, she said, "Julia Kimmel. I'm here with my little brother, Michael." She smiled reassuringly. Grown-ups love Julia.

As with our apartment, the elevator door opened right into the front hall. The difference between this place and our apartment, though, is that in our apartment, our bikes are lined up in the foyer, leaning against the mirror. Here, the floor was laid with marble, covered by a carpet so thick I felt like I was wearing new sneakers walking on it. The apartment smelled like lilies, a flower my mom hates because it reminds her of funerals.

A fragile, gray-haired woman emerged from the dark dining room. She was wearing a plaid wool skirt that fell below her knees. Her stockings were a little loose around her ankles, and she wore soft brown loafers and a thin sweater with a gold swirly brooch pinned over the breast. A charm bracelet dangled from one skinny wrist, and her hair was waved into puffs over her ears. She looked like my grandmother—not Stella, but the other one, Gaggy, who makes cookies and always has Life Savers in her pocketbook.

"You must be Michael," she said, looking straight at me. Her accent reminded me of the people around the farm my mom had grown up on in Connecticut—people who rhyme horse with floss. "I'm Charlisse Hillel-Broughton. I'm glad you decided to come."

Ewan was staring. "How did you know who he is?" he quizzed, like he was thinking maybe next she'd tell us all our favorite colors and where we hid our house keys.

"My doorman," she answered. "You were announced. And Laura Rosoff told me you might call."

Julia was standing straight-backed, her feet flexed into a tight first position. I could see her looking around the apartment approvingly. It looked like a museum, and Julia loves museums. In their puffy ski jackets, Gus and Trip looked like they were going to break something. "You've brought your friends," the woman said, still addressing me.

126

"Yeah," I said, wishing I knew a way to be more polite. *Yes? Yes, ma'am?* I thought of both of them too late. I pointed at Julia. "She's not my friend. She's my sister."

The woman gave a small, dry laugh. "Gallant for one so young," she said. I wasn't sure what she meant. She was hardly wider than my earth science textbook when she stood sideways. She smiled and I noticed that her eyes were bright and sort of pretty. Something made me want to look at them longer.

"What did Ms. Rosoff tell you about him?" Ewan asked.

"Please, come in," she said, still smiling as if all of this was more funny than it was real. "We'll sit down." She gestured into the dining room with an outstretched hand.

Julia swept in front of me. One of my arms swung dangerously near a sculpture that was a tower of crystal blocks with water trickling down into a small pool filled with stones. Ewan grabbed my sleeve just as I was about to follow Gus into the dining room. "Tell her everything," he said.

"You're sure she's real? She doesn't look like a psychic."

"What were you expecting, the cover of the Ouija box?"

"Kind of," I had to admit.

It was cold in the dark dining room, and while I rubbed my hands together, I looked around. Through three windows along one wall we could see bright blue sky. On our right, an arched door opened into a pink room where sofas and low armchairs were clustered in groups like in a hotel lobby. Past that room, through another arched door, I saw bookshelves and a dark rug, and beyond that was a room filled with light and plants.

The old lady beckoned for us to sit down at the polished mahogany table. I felt creeped-out and shy, and I was glad Trip and Gus were there. They looked just about as uncomfortable pulling out the carved wood chairs. I could see Julia rubbing the table with one appreciative finger. It was shiny enough to show her reflection.

"Laura Rosoff tells me, Michael, that she overheard you channeling a message from the dead father of your friend," the woman began.

"That was me," Ewan piped up.

"I didn't get a message exactly," I said. "It was just that suddenly, I was talking, and what I was saying made no sense."

"Yes," she said, smiling as if we were sharing a joke about the weather, or some misbehaving dog. "You will have no control at first."

"I—," I started. I had planned not to tell her everything right away, but I felt the story pushing against the back of my nose and eyes like a sneeze. "How can you do that?" I asked. "How can you make me want to tell you things?"

"You're noticing my way of seeing," she said. Once she said the word, I realized that's exactly what it felt like. She was seeing into me and pulling out what she wanted from inside my head. "I look at people and all I'm doing is paying proper attention to them," she went on. Her brown eyes crinkled.

"I don't believe in any of this," Gus interrupted.

"I'm not sure I do either," she laughed, turning to him. I could see his face relaxing the moment he met her eyes, just as mine must

128

have. "But the people I see," she went on, "they tell me it feels good. And I understand why. I'm looking for what stretches back to their parents, to things that are printed on their souls when they are very young, knowledge that you acquire before you know that you are acquiring knowledge, and before you learn to resist it." She looked back at me. "What way do you have of seeing?"

"I'm not really seeing," I said, and stopped there. It was like being thirsty, the way I wanted to tell her about Grandpa. And it was more than that. I felt a shifting of information in my mind, like there were pieces of thoughts stored in dusty boxes, and she was pressing buttons that put those boxes on conveyor belts and moved them to just behind my forehead. It was like my mom had let Mrs. Victor, our cleaning lady, do my room. I was finding things in cubbies and drawers I didn't even know had been lost. It did feel good.

"Call me Charlisse," she said.

"Okay," I said. "Charlisse." It felt weird calling her by her first name, but I'd already forgotten how to pronounce her last name, so it was convenient. "I see someone else's memories. I see inside them. And it's just one person, my grandfather. He's dead."

"Yes," she said, nodding her head as if I was saying things that were as normal as anything in the world.

"I slip—"

"Sleep?" I think she knew what word I meant but was giving me a chance to take it back.

"Slip," I said. "At least, Ewan calls it that. Slipping. I slip into a place my grandpa calls the river of the dead."

"What happens when you slip?" said Charlisse.

"He faints," said Gus. "I saw him."

"It's bad," Julia added. "He has convulsions. I think he needs to see a doctor."

"I get really cold," I said. "I feel my feet come out from under me. And then my body is moving through something that's really cold and clings to me and pushes on me all over. It makes me feel sad," I said, "and when I'm in it, I see inside my dead grandpa's memories. It's like I'm him, seeing things that he remembers."

It was embarrassing, telling so much of this. Especially the part about being sad. I don't know why that's so hard to say, but it is. "And then I stop feeling cold, and I kind of wake up and my dead grandfather—I didn't even really know him when he was alive—he takes me on a guided tour of other parts of his memories. We're standing inside the memories, and we're talking about them, and watching them all at the same time."

"Tell her about the touching," said Ewan. "How you could feel your grandpa this time."

"It's true," I said. "I couldn't feel him the first few times, but now, I think I might have started to."

Charlisse folded her hands on the table and looked down at them. As soon as her eyes let go of mine, I felt like I'd been standing in a nice warm shower that suddenly went cold. Not so cold that you have to get out, but cold enough so that it just kind of sucks.

Charlisse looked at her hands a long time. Ewan was staring at her worshipfully. Julia, Trip, and Gus were watching her too. Did they feel as lost as I did?

130

When Charlisse raised her head and looked straight at me again, I felt comfortable, safe, and warm. Her eyes—I really hadn't understood them before. They weren't bright. They were dark. Maybe she was frail in every place in her body, but her eyes made me think she'd be strong enough to pull me up a cliff by her pinkie.

"You are not a seer the way Laura Rosoff thought you might be," Charlisse said. "You might have the ability to become one, but for now, what's happening has more to do with the force of your grandfather's spirit than yours."

"Ewan says my grandpa's sucking out my life force. Do you think that's true?"

"Let me explain to you what I know," she said. "There is no hope of understanding if I give it to you in fragments. All right?"

"All right," I said. She looked at Ewan, who nodded, and then she turned her gaze to Julia, Trip, and Gus, each of whom nodded as well.

"Many ancient civilizations describe the world of the dead as a river," Charlisse began. "Or sometimes as a land you can only reach by crossing a river. But in all the legends, the river is always there. And mind you, these are very different civilizations we're talking about, civilizations that could not possibly have had any contact with one another. And yet they all came up with the same story. I believe the reason so many are in agreement is simple. They are right. The dead do form a river.

"We're born knowing this, but learn to reject the knowledge because none of us can see the river, and we have become slaves to the unforgiving requirement of science: proof. Though proof in this case would do no one any good. We return to our essential knowledge only through faith and trust. We attain truth only through the deepest meditation and study. And even then, we never see the truth but through a fog. One of the many great mystical texts calls it seeing 'through a glass darkly.'" She smiled wryly when Ewan raised his hand.

"Yes, Ewan," she said, with a look like she already knew what he was going to say.

"That's a quote from the Bible," he sputtered. "That's not a mystical text."

"I consider it to be one," Charlisse answered. "I'm aware that many people disagree with me. In any case," she went on, unlacing her fingers and laying them flat on the table, "many of the texts describe this river as lying beneath the earth. Which would make you think of sediment, shale, rock, lava, the tectonic plates that we know about today, all of which I'm sure you've learned about in school. So try to think of it this way: what the ancients were describing was not the earth our planet, but the earth our *home*."

I wasn't following her exactly, but I understood that she was saying the river was real. Which was scary, because she was a grown-up, and I think there was a part of me that had been pretty sure all the grown-ups who heard my story would insist to me that I had made it up, like Ms. Rosoff. I wanted to have made it up. But as long as she was speaking, and looking at me, I felt comfortable and warm. I trusted that I would soon understand.

"There's a philosopher named Plato you might have heard of who talked about the difference between something that is ideal and something that is real," Charlisse went on. "Do you know what I mean by ideal?"

"The best case?" said Julia.

"That's what it's come to mean," said Charlisse. "But Plato was talking about ideal as something that exists as an idea. Inside your head. If I say the word 'chair,' you see a chair in your mind. Does it look like the chair you're sitting in right now? No, because you're sitting in a real chair, and you're thinking of a simpler, basic chair. The ideal chair in your mind could be any chair and no chair at all. When I say 'a mother,' the picture you see in your mind is very different from when you think of your own mother, isn't it?"

"We don't get to Plato until AP English," Julia said, referring to the advanced placement classes Selden offered—they were hard, and counted for college.

Charlisse waved a hand in the air as if to dismiss the entire notion of AP. "The river of the dead is not a real river," she went on. "It's an idea of a river. It is an *ideal* river. There are no rock caves dripping with stalactites as so many painters have postulated. The river lives and flows inside of us. I like to think of it as a kind of water source for the plant life that is the human soul. It keeps us green and healthy. It nourishes us, and reminds us that we are part of something larger—something that connects all of us one to another."

Ewan raised his hand again. Charlisse kept hers flat and

relaxed on the table. I don't know if they were aware of it, but Trip and Gus had laid their hands flat on the table too.

"Listen only for now," Charlisse said, nodding in Ewan's direction. "You'll find you understand better when you trust that your questions will be answered. And they will be." She turned to me. "What I do," she said, "is descend to the edge of that river and stand still by its side."

I wasn't sure if she was expecting me to respond to this, but she was quiet for a minute, and I thought about how little she must look standing next to the river. I wondered if she was at the shore of the river, which suggested that the river had a surface. To me, it felt like you could swim and swim inside it forever and never reach the top.

"Have you ever known you were near the beach but not been able to see it?" she continued. "What do you hear? The waves. You feel moisture on your skin. You smell salt. If you know the spot, you can judge whether the tide is in or out based on the concentration of seaweed smell in the air."

I looked around at that moment at Gus and Trip. Was Trip hiding a smirk? His face showed nothing. Was Gus kicking him under the table? It didn't look like it. Wasn't someone going to interrupt Charlisse to say, "This is totally ridiculous. This can't be true." I wanted someone to. I wanted whoever that was to be right.

"What I do is inexact," Charlisse went on, "and it has taken me years to come as close to the river as I do. Still, as far from the river as I stand, it has changed me. I find myself struggling to pull back into this world. Standing at the river's edge is wonderful. It's death, but I don't feel alive anymore without it. It's why we love the ocean—it reminds us of this river we came from and will return to. But it's unnatural to know too much about it."

"And Michael is swimming in it!" Ewan interrupted, his sharp voice disturbing the calm. "Isn't he?"

Charlisse took a deep breath as if she wasn't quite ready to get there. "Yes," she said. "What Michael is doing is different from what I do. He is getting too close."

"Sometimes the dead pull someone into the river with them," she went on. "When there is a strong connection between two people, such as between a long-married couple, you'll often see one follow the other into death within a year of the first one's passing. This is actually a form of slipping—unbeknownst to those around them, the one who remains alive is going back and forth from the moment their beloved dies. They're so used to each other, they hardly realize what is going on. And when the second one dies, it's not a surprise. You see, most of us know about slipping without really knowing that we know. The married couple—in truth, they never were apart."

"But we didn't know my grandfather," Julia said. "How could he go six years without seeing us while he was alive, and then come back for Michael the moment he died, as if they had this great connection?"

"His desire," said Charlisse, "must be strong."

"But why?" Julia asked.

"Are you wondering," said Charlisse, "why the ghost of your grandfather didn't choose you?"

"No," said Julia, sounding so offended that I wondered for the first time if she *was* wondering that.

"It would be a very helpful question," Charlisse said, "if you were to wonder. Wondering will be what saves you. Pay attention to the questions you think to ask."

Julia seemed to recover a little of her dignity. "I don't know why Grandpa's doing anything," she said. "I don't know if I really believe any of this."

"But you do," said Charlisse. "You believe. Because you understand your grandfather. As does Michael. You know that once you discover what it is he is after, you will think, *Yes, I knew that all along.* You just can't articulate it now. Your challenge will be unlocking the knowledge."

"And you'll help?" Gus said. "Didn't you say that's what you do, help people find the knowledge they already carry around inside?"

Charlisse lifted her hands from the table and folded them. Somehow I knew that this gesture was a closing of a door. "In this case," she said, "Michael's access to the river running inside us is so much more powerful than mine, there is little I can do."

"He's having seizures," Julia said. "This is really dangerous. Mom and Dad should know."

Charlisse gently shook her head. "I know that you are children, and that what I am going to tell you now will seem a great shock. But you should try to see this situation from your parents' point of view. They will be—understandably—overwhelmed by fear. They will bring in doctors, counselors, even some incompetent practitioners of my own art. They will be trying to protect you, but what they will in fact be doing is imprisoning you, taking away your ability to focus on what you need to learn. You must tell them if you feel you have exhausted your own chances, but before you do that, I want you to understand what will happen if they know."

I looked down at the shining table. My hands were shaking. Inside this cold, formal palace of an apartment, under Charlisse's bright gaze, I was starting to actually believe that this was happening to me, that Charlisse was right, that there was a river, that I was swimming inside it.

"No way," said Trip. "There's always something that can be done. Is it money? My parents—"

Charlisse looked directly at me, and I felt my worry lie still. At the same time, Trip stopped talking in midsentence. I think he realized that this wasn't about money, which is weird, because when you live in New York, and when your family has as much money as Trip's does, I guess you don't hear that very often. He looked right at Charlisse, almost defiantly, but when she kept looking only at me, he lowered his gaze. I was starting to think that it didn't matter what Charlisse said. I had to tell Mom and Dad.

"Michael," Charlisse commanded. The strength of her voice matched the strength in her eyes. "Whatever it is your grandfather is looking for, you're the only one who can help him find it."

"What if I can't figure out what he wants?"

"It's not a question of whether you can figure it out," she said. "It's a question of whether you will or will not help him. I do hope you will, because if you don't, you will drown."

"Drown?" I said. "What are you talking about? Like, really drown?"

But Ewan was ahead of me, as always, asking a smarter question. "And if Michael does help his grandfather," Ewan said, "will he be okay?"

Charlisse looked old for the first time, and far away from us. "Maybe," she said. "Maybe not."

I felt again a rush of cold and fear. A sob was starting to block my throat. "*Maybe?*" I repeated. "Maybe *not?*"

"You should help us," said Julia. "This is crazy that a kid would have to do this on his own. It isn't fair."

"You're right," Charlisse said. "It isn't fair. But make no mistake. I am helping you. I am telling you what you need to know. You need to know that this is real. And that it's up to you children to solve it. And that I believe you can. But I can't do it for you. It will take all of you. All of your strength and wisdom and whatever self-knowledge you have managed to acquire in your young lives."

"Couldn't you go into a trance and visit Michael's grandfather in the river?" Ewan asked. "You said Michael can figure out what his grandpa wants, but what if he doesn't do it fast enough?"

"I could try to reach Michael's grandfather," Charlisse said, her voice softening so that we knew she was already pulling away from us. "But even if I knew what he wanted, I suspect Michael is the only one who can help him. His spirit reached out to Michael for a reason."

"I see," said Ewan, but in a way that sounded like he was just trying to think up his next question.

"I *don't* see," said Julia. She sounded like Dad when the super fixes the toilet and the next day it's leaking all over again. I couldn't believe she was talking to Charlisse this way—especially since Julia is always polite, especially to old, rich people. "I don't care if you're this great psychic. I don't care who you are or where you live. You should help Michael. You should do it right now."

"Julia," said Charlisse, speaking firmly, "I understand your concern. But Michael is not by himself. He is with you. And these friends. I am doing what I can, which I admit is very little—or very large, as it has taken a lifetime for me to acquire the knowledge that I give you today. But you have a part to play as well."

"What is it? What can I do?" Julia asked.

"I don't know the specifics," said Charlisse, and I think I saw Julia rolling her eyes. "But whatever part you have to play, you will play it well. You are strong, and you love Michael more than you may even know. That will help you to help him."

Julia opened her mouth to say more, but just then, her cell phone rang. She looked at the screen and pressed a button to make the ringing stop. "It's Mom," she said. "Michael, don't you want Mom to know what's going on?"

I thought about Mom. It was like I could see her in the room with me. Her short gray hair, her big eyes opening wide. One time, I had a fever so high, I lay awake at night certain there were trees growing inside the apartment. Mom held my hand. She rubbed a wet washcloth on my forehead. When she squeezed the water out of the washcloth into a bowl, I remember noticing the way her fingernails were cut down short. I could almost smell the lilac perfume she wears to parties and meetings.

But Charlisse was right. Mom would call Dad, and they would talk in low, serious voices, and then Mom would call doctors, and there would be meetings, and Dad would come to them, his cell phone ringing twenty times during each one. There would be whispering and secrets, but no one would believe that what I said was happening to me was real.

Gus was jiggling his left leg, shaking the table. "Whatever happens," he said, "I won't let you do this alone." I felt a shot of warmth flow into my body through my throat and warm me from the inside out. It was the opposite of the outside-in cold feeling of the river of the dead, and it made me feel like I understood things now. Like, being friends since first grade meant more than basketball. How could either of us have missed that?

"You believe me," I said, and it wasn't a question anymore.

"Yes," he answered. "I do."

"Thanks," I said, and I really meant it. "This has seemed kind of unreal up to now. Like you said before—a game. Like something that when there are other people around, doesn't count. Do you know what I mean?"

"It's real," Ewan said.

"It most assuredly is," Charlisse agreed. "You need to believe that, Michael. You need to listen. Pay attention, Michael."

"Great," I said. "Now you sound like my dad."

Charlisse smiled. "I know."

Chapter 13

"What now?" I said when we were standing on the bright wide sidewalk in front of Charlisse's building.

"Starbucks," Julia answered. "I need a latte, and we all need to talk." I guess I must have looked pretty freaked out, because after she'd met my eye, she said, "No one ever got sucked into a river of the dead in Starbucks."

But as soon as we were all sitting at a table by the window, I realized it was a mistake to come. Gus was doing what he always does at restaurants, folding his straw paper into an accordion and then suctioning liquid from his drink and releasing it onto the paper to make it wriggle on the table like a snake. Trip and Ewan were stirring their vente-whatevers with foot-long green straws. No one was talking. They were all waiting for me to come up with something to say.

What was I supposed to tell them? I just sat there. To be honest, I was wondering if I was going to burn my mouth on my hot chocolate or if it was safe to take a sip.

Ewan leaned forward, picked up a napkin, and began to fold it—in half, in quarters, in sixteenths, and thirty-seconds, until it was a wad. Holding it in his palm and watching it unfold on itself, he said, "So."

"Michael needs to think," said Trip. Was there anything he could say that wouldn't come out sounding like a threat? "About what his grandpa wants."

"Yes, Michael," said Julia. But then she made me feel really stupid by leaning back in her chair and crossing her legs, as if she knew this was going to be a while.

"Think," I repeated, as if by saying the word, I'd convince them I was doing it.

"You need to relax," said Gus. "If you try too hard, you'll never figure it out."

"Okay," I said, and repeated that word too: "Relax." Then I closed my eyes so they would at least think I was trying.

And I did try. I tried to block out of my mind how weird it was that I was here with Gus and Trip. Not to mention the weirdness of Julia and Ewan, and that we'd just met a real live psychic, and that she actually seemed to know what she was doing. I tried to block out the weirdness of not being able to talk to my mom, and the scariness of being away from Charlisse—I'd felt so safe there, and now I kind of felt like I was floating in space. I tipped back in my chair, balancing my hands on the slab of table in front of me. "What am I supposed to be thinking about again?" I said.

"Don't try to think about anything," said Gus. "Empty your mind."

"What are you, some kind of hypnotist?" said Trip. No one laughed.

"Try to remember Grandpa," prompted Julia. "What makes him happy? What makes him sad?"

Oh, yeah, I thought. *Grandpa.* Where *was* Grandpa? I didn't feel him with me anymore. Was he gone? I hadn't eaten any strange food in a while. The thought of the strange food—the spinach, the oatmeal—made me hungry. Grandpa had said I was going to like those foods for the rest of my life. Although maybe I wouldn't even *have* a rest of my life. How could Grandpa let something that bad happen to me? I knew he wouldn't. But even as I thought this, I was remembering how miserable it was in the tunnels in the river of the dead. He'd led me there, hadn't he? Still, I didn't think he would let me drown.

But even as I was thinking this, I was starting to feel just a little bit cold. It wasn't a river of the dead kind of cold feeling. It was just a little tingle of understanding, kind of like a shiver. It was enough, though, to make me feel Grandpa. I'm not sure how to explain this, but suddenly, I had him in my head, the way when you're trying so hard to remember a joke, and then you stop trying and the punch line comes to you.

I felt the front legs of my chair hit the floor, and then I was back in the memory of the time with Grandpa—just for a flash. The memory was of watching the girls laughing in the hallway of his college. That was happy, right? Except he'd seemed sad to be separated from them. And the way he talked about how he would stay in the city and work when my dad and Stella were up at the cabin? That was sad. All of it was kind of sad. "He's always sad, in a way," I said.

Everyone must have given up on me, because suddenly they all snapped back to attention.

"Sad how?" said Ewan.

"What do you mean, in a way?" asked Gus.

"Was he *ever* happy?" This last was Julia, and I decided to answer her first.

"Yes," I said. "He was almost always a little happy too."

"How could he be both?" asked Gus.

"I don't know," I said. "It's like he was enjoying seeing everything but wishing it had been different. I think he didn't like the way the story came out." That sounded pretty smart, I thought. I was thinking: *that should hold them awhile.* But they didn't stop.

"What story?" Ewan asked.

"The story of his life," I said. "The war, Grandma's dying when she was young."

Julia cleared her throat. When she spoke, her voice was small. "Was he sad about you?"

"He didn't even know me," I said.

Before Julia could answer, Trip blurted out, "My therapist says men always trace things back to their fathers."

"Your *therapist?*" I said. Trip went red in the face, from his neck right up through his forehead.

"My mom . . . my brothers . . . ," he stammered. "Look. My mom said no allowance until my brothers and I go. Ever since my dad, you know—"

"Went to jail?" Julia finished.

"Yeah," said Trip. He started cracking his knuckles. "Good

old Dr. Chinois." He was fiddling with the lid from his frappucino, and suddenly he tore it in half. No one knew what to say.

Except Ewan. "I go to Dr. Chinois," he piped up. Trip looked over at him, and I could see his face relaxing, the eyebrows settling back down to their normal position. Ewan was smaller and weaker than Trip, but I was starting to see that he was also braver.

"You do?" Trip said.

"He's an expert on kids with father issues," said Ewan. "It's the basis for his practice, taking the focus off mothers in the therapy of boys."

"But Grandpa never talks about his father," I said.

Julia cleared her throat and took a sip of her latte—she's such a grown up, she doesn't even use sugar. "You know the big fight he and Dad had?" she said. "Do you know what it was about?"

"No," I said.

"It was about you."

"They were both mad at me?" I said.

"Dad wasn't mad at you," Julia said. "He was trying to protect you. The last time we went up there, when Mom and Dad were out somewhere, you told Grandpa it was really boring at his house and that you didn't want to visit anymore."

"It was boring," I said, mumbling because now that I knew Grandpa, I wished I hadn't said that.

"Grandpa got really mad," Julia said. "He gave us a giant lecture about how when he was a child he would have been grateful to be able to play in the woods, how he grew up in the city, where no one got to swim in lakes or play on the grass. And he wouldn't let you play outside all afternoon to teach you what it was like to live in an apartment."

"But we already lived in an apartment," I said.

"I know," Julia said. "When Mom and Dad came back, Dad made that point. He was even more mad than Grandpa. I guess you don't remember this, but he and Grandpa—there was always some big yelling when we were up there. About the littlest things, like Dad wanting to cook steak and Grandpa saying it was too expensive even though Dad said he would pay for it."

"Really?" I said. I didn't remember that at all.

"One time," she went on, "I remember hiding in the sleeping loft, listening to them shouting about Dad's work. Grandpa was making it sound like Dad's clients were a bunch of criminals, and Dad was trying to make a fire in the woodstove, and it wasn't lighting, and the whole time he was running through a list of all his clients, saying why they deserved to be defended, and the fire still wasn't lighting, and Grandpa was just sitting there, not saying anything, and Dad was getting madder and madder. I don't know where you were then. Maybe you were with Mom.

"But the last time—the time Grandpa locked you in the cabin for the afternoon—Dad didn't just storm around. He made Mom pack up our stuff and put you and me in the car. I could hear him, he was yelling at Grandpa, saying, 'You don't have the right to teach my children any lessons!' and Grandpa said, 'How dare you!' They were both bellowing. After a few minutes, Mom came out to the car and sat with us, and what I remember most is that she was crying."

"I don't remember that at all," I said.

"Yeah, I think you fell asleep," Julia said.

"I fell asleep?" I said. "During a fight that was so bad Dad and Grandpa stopped speaking to each other forever?"

"You were just as oblivious then as you are now."

"What do you mean, oblivious?" I said. That made me sound like such a loser. "I'm not oblivious. You're just trying to make yourself seem smarter than me. You're just jealous."

"Oh, please," said Julia. "I'm not jealous of you. I'm just trying to tell you. It's like what Dad's always saying. You just don't look around you. When Mom's super-busy, or Dad's in a bad mood, you just sit there playing video games."

"You're the one who's oblivious," I said. "All you do is ballet."

"That's different."

"No, it's not."

Gus jumped in. "Guys, cut it out. Julia, finish the story."

Julia folded her hands primly in her lap. I thought she was only pretending she wasn't still mad. "When Dad got in the car, we drove home," she said. "He wouldn't talk, even to Mom."

"And that's it?" said Trip. "He stopped talking to his own father because Michael got punished?"

"Generally, Dad loves for me to be punished," I said.

"What do *you* think he wants?" Ewan asked Julia.

"I don't know," she said, resting her chin in her hands. She wasn't mad anymore. When people are mad, I've noticed, they have a hard time relaxing their bodies into thinking positions. That was so typical of her—to say something mean about me but not even mean to be mean. To not even realize what it feels like not to be exactly perfect.

"Are you even listening, Michael?" she said. "All this time, you're kind of spacing out. It's like you don't even care that you're in danger."

"I care," I said.

"Then try to figure out what's happening," she said. "Grandpa picked you. Remember that. Charlisse said it was important. He didn't pick Ewan, Trip, or Gus, and he didn't pick me. I'm not jealous, Michael. I'm worried. You have to start paying attention."

"He should have picked you," I said, because she was right. I wasn't going to be able to do this. "You would have figured this whole thing out by now."

I could see in her eyes that she agreed with me, but at least she didn't say that out loud. She just sat back in her chair and let Ewan keep taking us through the story of what had happened, looking for clues as to what Grandpa wanted. We went around in circles, and didn't solve anything.

At six o'clock, we knew we had to leave Starbucks or Mom would start to really worry. Before we left, we made a plan. Julia had a dress rehearsal for *Sleeping Beauty*. Julia and I would go home. I would cover the mirrors and windows in my room, and not leave. Ewan, Gus, and Trip would tell their mothers they were working on a report, and go to Gus's apartment, where Gus had high-speed Internet and Ewan could do more research. We'd meet the next morning at Gus's house at ten.

I told my mom I wasn't feeling well, and she ordered a pizza and I ate it in my room while she and Julia were out at rehearsal. It was really boring to have no TV (it's a reflective surface), no Xbox (again, reflective), or even a Game Boy to play with (it's like a pocket mirror—I'd never noticed that before). But it was kind of a cool feeling to have the windows covered with sheets. In New York, light comes in at night from the streetlights and the apartments across the way. With the windows covered up, I could have been anywhere. I skipped brushing my teeth to avoid the bathroom mirror, and kept my eyes closed when I peed (sorry, rug).

As I was going to sleep—insanely early, like, nine!—I remembered that I was supposed to figure out stuff about my grandpa. But I was too tired to think. I wondered how long I was going to have to go without playing video games. Maybe Ewan would have something new figured out by morning. Or Julia. The strange thing about slipping was that even though I was scared a lot of the time, there was something kind of cool about having all these people helping me. I was sure that tomorrow they'd work together to figure something out.

This is what actually happened:

I woke up to my dad saying, "Start brushing." He was sitting on the edge of my bed, holding my toothbrush, already smeared with Crest. I remembered this trick from the few times we'd actually gone on vacation as a family—lame road trips meant to take the place of longer, more exciting vacations far away. My dad hated to wait around in the mornings. He made us stay in those hotels where you park right outside the door to your room because it meant he could pack up while everyone was still sleeping and we wouldn't get in his way.

"What time is it?" I said now. "What are you doing here?"

"It's five thirty," he said. "I'm going to Vermont today. I'm taking you with me."

"To Vermont?" I said. I was still half asleep.

"We have to deal with Grandpa," he said. "And the cabin."

"What about school?"

"Good point, except it's Saturday."

"Julia!" I called, because by now I was awake enough to know that she was the only person in shouting distance who knew what the danger was.

"Shhh." My dad clapped a hand over my mouth. "She was up until all hours last night. She and Mom are staying for *Sleeping Beauty* rehearsals. Don't wake her up."

I stared at him. I had no idea what to do.

"This feels like you're kidnapping me," I said.

"Start brushing," he replied. I did.

An hour later, I was locked in the passenger seat of my dad's Mercedes. The sun had not yet come up. As the bumpy expressways that run right up next to apartment buildings widened into the well-lit highways of the suburbs, I ran through all the things I should have said back in the apartment—that I was sick, that I would stay with Gus. I even wished I'd told my dad the truth, because the worst part about sitting on the slippery leather seat of my dad's car was that I was alone with the knowledge of what might happen to me.

Or maybe that was the second-worst part. I reclined my seat, lay back, crossed my arms, and waited for the car to get warm, or for the toothpaste coating my teeth to dissolve, or something. The one thing I can say about how gross I felt from having gotten out of bed without being fully awake was that at least I was too sleepy to be scared.

As the houses and shopping malls fell away, the sun began to rise. My dad turned on a rebroadcast of a basketball game. "If you know what happened, don't tell me," he said, and I shrugged. I didn't know. The announcer's voice crackled away above the station's static. Ewan and Julia, even Trip or Gus, couldn't help me now.

I must have fallen asleep, because I woke up to find the car stopped. I pulled myself to a sitting position and looked out the window—we were at a gas station, and my dad was pumping gas. We weren't on a major highway, just a two-lane road that was brown from road sand and dusty with snow blowing off the banks that had been made by a plow. Because there was so much snow blowing around, a thin line of it had been trapped on top of the pumps.

As I was thinking that the light on the snow reminded me of the light inside the river of the dead, my dad was coming back from the cashier's window, where he'd just paid. A wind came up and he was engulfed by a swirl of white blowing between the pumps and the office. For a second, inside the swirling snow, my dad looked far away, and paler, like he'd faded into an old man with pink skin and white streaks in his hair.

signs with their names on them—half to the left, half to the right. One of the signs was labeled KIMMEL. It was strange to see a name I thought of as belonging to my family posted to a tree in the middle of the woods in Vermont. As much as I'd come to know Grandpa as a ghost, it was weird to think that he had been part of the same real-life family with the name Kimmel when he was alive.

But when we entered the clearing where the cabin stood, our visits here started coming back. The window trim was still painted bright red, and the cabin had a tin roof that was dark green, like the needles on the tall pines. It didn't look like the cabin in Grandpa's early memory—I think the roof then was black, and the woods had not grown up.

I'd never seen the cabin in the snow. Back when we used to come, it was always summer, though sometimes summer was so cold we had to wear sweaters and light the woodstove at night. I remember once being half awake when we got to the clearing. Grandpa had stepped out of the front door and looked at us without smiling or waving, like someone in an old-fashioned photograph where they had to hold the same expression for three minutes or else their face would look like a blur.

Now, because of the snow, my dad had to leave the car out on the road. Opening the door, he took his first step, and fell in up to his thigh. "Careful, Michael," he said to me. I slid across the seat after him. I had to sort of jump down into the holes he'd made. I followed him one giant leap at a time to the porch, where wood was stacked all the way up to the ceiling, just as I remembered, and covered in a bright blue tarp tied down with ropes. Dad was wearing his weekend dress shoes, which were some kind of soft leather slip-on things my mom buys him. "Didn't you bring boots?" I said to him.

"I forgot. It's been a while since I left New York."

"Yeah." I showed him my sneakers. "Me too."

We stomped our feet to shake off the snow, but a lot of it had already melted inside our shoes and along our legs. After trying the door and finding it locked, my dad pulled out a set of keys inside a yellowed envelope—I guess he must have been holding on to them all these years—and started to sort through them in his freezing hands. I stepped in front of him, jiggled the front door to the left, and it opened.

"How did you know to do that?" Dad asked.

I shrugged. "Lucky guess."

There wasn't much light coming through the windows into the cabin, but there was enough to see that the one big room had not changed. A table with two chairs atop a braided rug filled the center of the room. Along a far wall lay a single bed. Behind me was the short countertop with a sink, fridge, and a small gas cooking range.

The cabin didn't look like Grandpa was dead. It looked like he'd just stepped out. His bed was unmade, a thick wool blanket and a quilt pushed down to the bottom of the mattress. A pair of brown leather boots, well-creased at the toe, with black and red striped laces stood next to the door. Split wood was piled next to the woodstove. The only sign that he'd been gone awhile was a mug of coffee out on the table, the milk marbled, going bad.

My legs ached with cold, and I felt my teeth begin to chatter. "It looks like he just left," I said. "Not like he died."

"He'd been waiting half his life to die." My dad lifted the envelopes in the pile of mail to see who they were from.

"Can you light a fire?" I asked. "I'm freezing."

"I don't want to have to wait for it to burn out," Dad said. He found a box of trash bags under the sink. "We'll get warmer the faster we work." He handed me a bag, and said, "Everything in the fridge. All the food in the cabinets that's already opened." I did what he told me to, dropping into the bag a half-full jug of the milk I remember him mixing from powder, an egg carton with three eggs in it, a container of tuna salad, two rotting oranges, a tub of butter, lettuce, a pale pink tomato. Soon the bag was too heavy to carry, and I dragged it across the floor.

"Let me have that," said Dad, "it's going to leak."

I made a move to sit down on the bed. "Keep going," Dad said. "It's the only way to stay warm."

He was right. After throwing out all the food, we filled garbage bags with clothing and old magazines. We filled boxes with dishes and pots and pans, pencils and china bowls. We packed up the dirty towels in the bathroom, and the worn-down bathroom rug. Anything not perishable got stacked by the door. My dad put all the garbage in the trunk of his car, and anything we wanted to keep in the backseat—he said Goodwill would come for everything else. Stepping gingerly in the holes in the snow, he dragged one bag after another behind him. Even being careful, his pant legs were white with snow when he came back in, and pretty soon, he showed me how his pants were growing stiff as the water logged in the fabric was turning to ice.

As we worked, I felt the air in the cabin beginning to change. It reminded me of how Grandpa said the air smelled sweeter when we were together, but it wasn't sweet that I was smelling, it was sad, if you can call that a smell—it was a damp, musty odor tinged with a hint of rot.

With each breath, I felt like I was letting more and more sadness into my body, and the sadness was gathering there, squeezing at my heart, making me feel as if I was going to cry. I wasn't crying. Not yet. But how was I supposed to be figuring out what Grandpa wanted from me when my dad was making me put everything that had belonged to Grandpa in the trash?

After a few hours, the cabin didn't look like anyone lived in it anymore. The mattress was stripped of sheets, and we could see how it was stained and lumpy. The curtains had been so old, they ripped as we tried to pull them closed. My dad said, "My mom must have put these here," in a tone that sounded halfway between disdain and wonder. With the curtains removed from the windows, we could see that they were dirty—hardly any light came through. We could hear the wind blowing outside. What had it been like to live here, winter after winter, all alone?

When I looked over at my dad, wondering if he was thinking the same thing, he was holding Grandpa's toothbrush. It was a red toothbrush with bristles that were curled and worn, and I saw him look at it for a second. I thought, Maybe he's going to feel sad, and just the idea of his feeling sad made me feel sad. But then my dad didn't feel sad. Or at least, he didn't look sad. He chucked the toothbrush into the garbage bag as if it were an animal that had bitten him. He swept Grandpa's denture cleaning kit into the trash as well—I'd looked at it before but hadn't wanted to go near it. Briskly, Dad tied a knot in the top of the bag and carried it out to the car.

He came back with the cardboard box holding my grandfather's ashes. He put the box on the table, as if it would replace the salt and pepper shakers and sugar bowl we'd emptied and put in the box for Goodwill. It was getting dark, though it was still mid-afternoon. Dad hadn't turned on any lights except the one over the sink, so the box was in shadow.

"Okay," he said, clapping his hands together like a camp counselor. How could he sound so cheerful? "I think we're done here. We're going to turn off the fridge and the water and the gas. Did you know you could do that to a house?"

I could feel the first sob coming, so I watched him turn a dial in the back of the empty fridge without saying a word. He explained that you leave the door open to keep mildew from forming, and you shut off water under the sink, then run the water out of the taps in the kitchen and bathroom until they are dry to keep water from freezing inside the pipes.

Didn't he care that Grandpa loved him? Didn't he know how Grandpa had been watching him all those times and just couldn't find the right words to break through? When Dad had been practicing diving off the float in the lake, Grandpa had been proud. When he'd been doing his homework in his room, Grandpa had wanted to touch his shoulder, had wanted to say to him, "That's my boy."

My fingers were aching and my nose was starting to run. I was so cold, all I wanted to do was get back in the car, turn the heater up to high, and put my hands and face directly down on a vent. But when Dad turned to leave without even looking back, I couldn't follow. We'd taken apart Grandpa's whole life in one afternoon, and we were leaving all that was left of his body alone in a cold, dark cabin where he had never once been happy all his life. We were leaving Grandpa behind without saying good-bye.

"Dad, wait," I said. I could hear my voice beginning to crack. I didn't want to cry. I didn't want him to see I was sad. What I wanted him to see was that *this* was sad. What was this? I couldn't say exactly. All I could come up with was, "You forgot Grandpa's ashes."

"Yes?" said my dad.

"Um, are you sure we shouldn't bring the box back home with us?"

"No, we'll leave it here."

"Aren't we going to bury him?"

"Not now."

"What if the cabin gets broken into?"

"This is Vermont," said my dad. "That's not how it works up here."

"What if it's broken into by a bear?"

"Then I feel sorry for the bear."

"This isn't funny! You can't just leave someone's ashes in an empty cabin," I said.

"Are you crying?" Dad asked.

"No," I said, and then, "It's your fault."

"What? You're mad at me?"

"No," I said, but I was. "Why couldn't you have been nicer to Grandpa? Why did you stop speaking to him? Why did you never come back?"

"You want *me* to have been nicer to *him?*" Dad sat down on a chair next to the table, as if this question were so shocking he had to steady himself. "Michael," he said, "I don't know what's gotten into you since my father died, but let me make something absolutely clear to you right now. I know my father had a hard life in a lot of ways, growing up with money tight. I know he had a hard time in the war. But he was a horrible father. I don't think he wanted to have a kid. My mother died when I was young, and after she was gone, I think he tried as much as he could to never speak to me. After I left home, he didn't try to get me to come back. I visited him for years with almost no encouragement. He didn't want me—he didn't want us, do you understand? He didn't want people. He didn't want a family. He didn't have those feelings."

"What if he did?" I said.

"You didn't know him," my dad corrected. "You weren't there. Maybe it's hard for you to imagine because you don't have a father like this, but I know. He was there with his body, but in other ways, he was always gone." He stood up. "It's freezing. We can talk about this more in the car, but we need to get going. If we don't leave soon, we won't be able to get home tonight."

"I'm not leaving him here," I said.

160

"And I'm not taking him with me," said my dad. "I don't want him in my house. I don't want him in my life."

"I do," I said.

My dad stood over me, towering. "Michael," he said, in his sternest, most serious voice, pointing to the door. "Get in the car."

"No," I said. "I'm not leaving." I didn't know what I wanted to say next, and I'm not sure where this came from, but "You're just like him!" kind of poured out of me.

My dad's face went white, and I felt a shiver of recognition. I was right. All those protein shakes instead of dinner. Grandpa standing outside my dad's room trying to think of something to say. Dad and Grandpa were the same. Dad was pretending—he'd always been pretending—that he was different. Even the last few days—the family dinner, the basketball practice. He'd been forcing himself. "You try to act like you're not like him," I said, "like you're this great dad, but you're not. You don't want me either. You don't even like me. You don't like my hair, you don't think I try hard enough in school. You don't like it when I play video games. You never want to talk to me. Grandpa talks to me. He's the only one who ever listens to what I have to say."

"What are you talking about?" Dad said.

If I'd been more rational, maybe I would have understood his confusion. But just then, what I was thinking was that it was my dad's fault that I'd started slipping in the first place. I was thinking that Grandpa was really coming back to get my dad, but he couldn't, because my dad didn't feel anything—there hadn't been a way to get in. So Grandpa had come to me.

161

"Get in the car, Michael," my dad said. He was still standing over me, still pointing to the door. "The things you're saying are hateful and rude. I'm telling you, I'm serious, there is going to be hell to pay if you do not walk out that door, get in the car, and shut up this exact minute."

I was scared. My dad is a lot bigger than me. And he doesn't ever say things like "shut up" or "hell." But I didn't move. "Look at me," I said to my dad.

"What?" he said, but while he waited for me to answer his question, I locked into his eyes with my own, and stared as hard as I could.

"What are you doing?" he said.

I didn't answer, just kept looking at him and concentrating. The first time I'd slipped, Grandpa had said something about my eyes, how he'd seen Grandma in them, and got to me that way. That's what I was trying to do now.

My dad—what did I see there? His eyes were just like mine, brown on the outside, and yellow green near the pupil. As I held his gaze, they changed, his eyes, like he was thinking, and then they started to get wet, like they do when you try not to blink. Looking back, I wonder if I was doing something to him like Charlisse had done to me—making me feel like I was standing on solid ground, making me not want to look away, to be thirsty for what I was seeing in her eyes.

And that's when it happened. If I hadn't been looking for Grandpa, I would never have known what I was seeing. First, it was a fleck of white—the tip of Grandpa's white hair. Then there was a tiny something that might have been the pink of his skin. Just those two hints of Grandpa, and I started to feel cold. Or colder. I was already a regular kind of cold. My legs were getting heavy, and I must have sat down hard on the floor. I felt a shock of pain on my butt, but it was really far away. I wasn't ready. But I was going in.

"Michael!" Dad said. "Are you all right?" His voice came from far away, and he looked tiny but totally clear, like the gym lockers I'd seen at the end of the tunnel before. I tried not to hold on against the slip, I tried not to grab at the edge of the cliff.

I could see out of my half-closed eyes that my father was trying to make a call into his cell phone, even though there wasn't service.

"Michael!" he shouted, and I remembered the way Grandpa used to shout "Michael!" when he was chopping wood and wanted me to stand back. I felt his alarm, his worry. I saw the image that he'd seen in his mind, of the ax falling on a little boy's arm, the terrible act that cannot be taken back. The Grandpa I knew then was different from the Grandpa of now, and yet the way he had shouted was just like my dad, and like himself too.

The last thing I remember was my dad standing at the window. "I think I see a car," he said. "I'm going out to stop it. Michael, hold on!"

But I was already gone.

Chapter 14

This time I didn't travel through any of Grandpa's memories as I tunneled through the river of the dead. I think it might have been because I was moving faster, so fast I didn't have time to see what I was passing through. And my guess is that I was moving faster because the tunnel was now wider. Ewan had said that as the slips happened the connection expands. Whatever it was I was tunneling through, it was still cold, but I didn't feel it squeezing against my body. As I slipped this time, I could still breathe.

I woke up on Grandpa's bed in the cabin, with Grandpa sitting next to me. The cabin looked the way Dad and I had found it when we came in earlier, and there was a fire burning in the woodstove. Grandpa was holding a mug of something that was steaming, which he handed to me when he saw that I was awake.

"It's cocoa," he said. I took a sip, and there was something warm about the drink even though I couldn't exactly feel or taste it. The tingling at the roof of my mouth reminded me of the feeling I'd had when I touched Grandpa's shoulder back at the lake.

"Grandpa," I said, "I've figured out what's wrong. I think I know what you're looking for."

I was expecting him to raise his eyebrows and look eager for my news, but instead his face kind of collapsed. Grandpa shook his head. "You shouldn't have come back here," he said. "It's dangerous for you. I've been trying not to reach you. It's like holding your breath, you know, it's horrible, but I've been doing it. You found me this time."

"It's okay," I said. "I've talked to a lot of people who know all about what's happening and they told me how to fix it. It's like a video game. You have to figure out what you need to get to the next level. And I know now. I know what you need." This should have been good news for him. Why was he still looking sad?

"You see," I started in again, "you told me about the shell around your heart. Well, my dad has one too. That's why he doesn't cry. And doesn't feel hungry—that's why he can eat protein shakes instead of actual food. It's why he works all the time like you did." My voice trailed off. Why wasn't this making the kind of sense out loud that it had made inside my head?

Grandpa was watching the door. "I'm sorry, Michael," he said. "It's too late. Last time . . ." He shifted off the bed to standing. He looked at the door.

"Last time what?" I said.

"Last time, when you touched my shoulder," he began. He turned to look at me, and I saw that even though he was a ghost and couldn't produce real tears, his eyes were full and shining. "I felt your hand. And just now, you could taste the cocoa, couldn't you?"

"Yes," I said. "A little."

"I don't think that's good," he said. "I think maybe it means you're beginning to do more than visit this place."

I put the mug down. Suddenly, I didn't want to know if it might be getting warmer, which indeed it was. "I just thought," I said. Grandpa furrowed his brow. "I thought I'd figured it out. I thought I was finally paying attention to things. I thought I had a chance. I wasn't supposed to get stuck. Not yet."

Grandpa took a step toward me and tousled my hair. A feeling of dread settled into my stomach at the knowledge that I could more than kind of feel his hand on my head. It was also weird to think that all during the time that he was alive, I don't remember his touching me.

"Michael," he said, "let's try to get you out of here. Right now."

"But what about you? I'm supposed to try to help you."

"Don't worry about me. The longer you stay, the worse this will be."

"Okay," I said, feeling small.

"Give me your hands," Grandpa said. Together, we sat down on the edge of the bed. But just then, the door to the cabin opened, and a version of Grandpa who looked almost exactly the same as Ghost Grandpa walked into the room. Covered in a dusting of snow, he carried a piece of firewood in each hand.

"Oh, no," said Grandpa. "Oh dear," he said, and then, "Oh dear *me*. I don't think you should see this."

"See what?" I said. It didn't look like we were seeing anything particularly exciting. The still-alive version of Grandpa closed the door to shut out the swirling snow. He tossed the firewood he was carrying onto a pile next to the stove. He bent over to undo the red and black striped laces on the brown boots and left them in the spot where my dad and I would find them later. He was wearing a string around his neck, and there was a piece of plastic the size of a quarter hanging off it, with a red button in the center. I recognized the necklace from a TV ad showing old people falling out of their recliners and using the button to call an ambulance.

"This is the oldest I've ever seen you. Was this after we stopped coming to visit?" I said.

"Yes," said Grandpa. "It was morning. I'd just finished bringing in the last load of firewood. I had enough piled up to get me through to the end of the day." He sighed and put a hand on my shoulder. This time, instead of tingling, I felt something solid behind his touch. Not fingers, not a palm, but something.

"Grandpa," I said, "I can feel you really well."

"Look how tired I was," he said. The still-alive Grandpa sat down in a chair at the table. "My body was ready to go, but the idea of dying still scared me. It was as close then as it was during the war. Back in the war—phew!—it was all any of us thought about. No one talked about it, but I couldn't eat because of how scared I was. Of course, eventually, the idea of dying stopped feeling as important as the idea of getting something hot into my stomach. That was because I'd started to build up the shell. I needed a nice thick shell, and boy, oh, boy did I get it. And kept it with me."

Grandpa talking about dying was giving me an uncomfortable suspicion. "Grandpa," I said, "didn't you say you wanted to take me back? We were touching before—shouldn't that have started it?"

"Yes," he said, snapping back to attention. "It should have. Maybe we weren't touching for long enough. We'll try it right now." He placed both hands on my shoulders.

"Shouldn't we say good-bye?" I said.

He lifted his hands and held them in his lap for a moment. He took a breath as if he was about to speak, and then he closed his lips tight.

"No," he said. "We can't. I can't bear to. Is that too horrible?" He looked so anxious and so pained, I couldn't tell him that yes, I thought it was weird.

"It's okay," I said. "Let's go."

He put his hands back on my shoulders. I closed my eyes and braced myself for the cold.

But as I sat there waiting, and waiting some more, I realized that I wasn't getting colder at all. "What's wrong?" I said, opening my eyes.

"I don't know," he replied, shaking out his arms before laying them on my shoulders again. "I'll try again." He closed his eyes again, and again, I braced myself for the cold. Nothing happened. "Usually, I just let go," Grandpa said. "Usually, slipping back into the river is easy, even if it's a little hot each time. It feels like I have nothing to do with it."

"Hot?" I said. "It's freezing!"

168

"Shh," he said, and started taking shallow breaths through his nose, closing his eyes this time.

But his concentration was broken by the whistle of a kettle on the stove. We both watched the other Grandpa rise from the table and move slowly to lift the kettle off the flame. We smelled the coffee as the hot water hit the grounds, and Ghost Grandpa breathed in through his nose. "Delicious," he said. We watched the Alive Grandpa shuffle back to the table and set the mug down.

He pulled a piece of paper and a pen from a drawer in the table and sat over them, taking a small sip from the coffee cup, lifting the pen, and then putting it down again.

"What were you doing?" I asked.

"Writing a letter."

"Who were you writing to?"

"To your dad. I tried writing to him nearly every day."

"Did he ever write back?"

"He never got the letters. I never sent them."

"Oh," I said.

Grandpa laughed, a dry little cough, and it was so full of sadness I realized I had been feeling sad myself. I was learning that feeling sad and feeling cold have a lot in common, and just as I was thinking that, I understood what I was going to see.

Charlisse had told me to pay attention, and I had. I knew the coffee Grandpa wasn't drinking would stay right where it was on the table, in the same chipped blue mug. The fire that was crackling now would die out, and Dad and I would sweep those ashes into the tin bucket sitting next to the woodstove.

The boots with the well-creased toe, the red and black laces that looked like someone had just taken them off—they would look just that way when I found them. And the unmade bed I was sitting on right now, these were the sheets and blankets Dad and I would fold.

"Grandpa," I said, hardly able to make a sound.

Grandpa couldn't look at me. "I'll get you out of here," he said. "I promise. I don't know why it isn't working. You shouldn't see this!"

"Keep trying," I said, because now that I knew what was ahead, I wanted to get out of there more than he wanted me to go. I gave him my hands and breathed like him, trying to will myself into another place.

It didn't work. We tried again. We tried and tried until I started to feel Grandpa's hands shake.

"No," I said. "We can't be stuck here. Come on!" I grabbed Grandpa's hand, pulling for the door. So strange that I could touch him for real now. He didn't feel cold to me at all.

But he wouldn't move. "Michael, stop," he said. "It's no good."

"The porch!" I shouted, letting go of his stubborn hand to cross the room, passing the still-alive Grandpa, with his pen and paper and cup of coffee. "Come on." Why didn't he understand that if we were on the porch, we wouldn't have to see?

When I opened the door, I saw why. For outside, there wasn't the snowy day that we'd been watching out the window. The air was black. And it wasn't really air. It felt like what happens when

170

you hold two magnets up against each other. It was a great pushing, a force against me. It was too stiff for me to put an arm or even a finger out into it, and I wondered if, like a magnet, some things might get sucked into it hard and fast. I couldn't see into the blackness, but I could feel that it went on and on—and down and down. I was afraid of the air that wasn't air. I'd been standing in front of it just a second before I felt a burning inside my nose from the cold, and a stinging on the skin of my arms. There was wind too. I could hear it.

I had to lean against the door with my whole body before it would close. "What was that?" I said to Grandpa. He looked up at me and swallowed hard.

"Tell me," I said, because I knew he didn't want to.

"It's the river," he said, his voice small. "Or the light. The darkness. Whatever you want to call it. But it's changed."

"Can't we just push through it?" I said. "Like we usually do?"

"No," Grandpa said. "If we can't get into the river, it must mean that the energy is gone, or is fading." His face twisted with sadness. "Michael," he said. "Come here. Be with me. It's about to start."

I took a few steps back across the cabin toward him. There was a noise behind me, and I turned to see Alive Grandpa pushing back in his chair. Half standing, he was grabbing his left arm, and then he was stumbling across the room. I had to step out of his way, and I felt Ghost Grandpa's hands pulling me back toward the bed. Alive Grandpa was leaning on the kitchen counter. With one shaking hand, he pressed the button on the string

171

around his neck. Then he struggled across the room, bracing himself against the backs of chairs, just missing putting his hand on the hot woodstove. He half made it to the bed but fell to the floor before he could reach it. Ghost Grandpa and I had to move backward quickly to avoid him.

The old man lay on the floor, his arms to his sides, his clear brown eyes open and staring into the cabin's rafters.

I was so scared, I let Ghost Grandpa pull me onto his lap, like I was a little boy. His touch was as definite as if we were both alive and real in the world.

While Alive Grandpa lay on the floor in front of us, Ghost Grandpa started talking very fast, like he had a lot to say to me in a very short amount of time. "I want you to know," he whispered into my ear, "I love you more than I loved my life. I love you the way I loved your father, I loved Stella, I loved my own mother, my father, your sister, Julia. I built that shell around my heart to protect myself from the love. When you've lived much of your life in fear, it's hard to feel love without also feeling fear—fear that you'll become a slave to the love, fear that love will ruin or desert you, fear that you will have to one day live without love again. But now I'm afraid my love for you is hurting not me, but you. I've dragged you in here with me and you're going to have to share my pain—oh, Michael, I'm so sorry!"

"No," I breathed, because even though I felt a sour black taste come into my mouth, I could feel Grandpa's hot whisper in my ear, and I could feel his arms around mine. Gone was the cold of his touch. There were times when he was talking when I couldn't separate his breath and voice in my ear from my own living thoughts. He was so close to me, we were the same.

"Michael," Grandpa said, "I think when I was dying, something happened to me. Time went very slowly. While I was waiting to go, I saw everything. Stella. Daniel—your father. The war. My years up here. The shell I'd built up around my heart cracked open, and all the memories came flooding back. I lay there and I couldn't move, and I was so, so sorry." Grandpa was squeezing me hard. "There was nothing I could do. There wasn't anything that could save me. It wasn't like the time in the war—when I saw you playing basketball—or maybe it was myself I saw then? Repeating, we're all repeating ourselves, aren't we? This time, I didn't see anyone to help me. I couldn't reach. I couldn't change a thing."

"This was how you died?" I asked. It couldn't be like this, I thought. That you could be sitting at a table, perfectly normal, and then the next second lying on the floor, and then not too long after that, be gone. I didn't want Grandpa to go. "You were just lying there, all alone?"

The man on the floor groaned. "Oh, Stella, I'm sorry," he said aloud. "Oh, Daniel." His voice had so much pain and sadness in it, I thought something inside me might break.

"I was remembering all my chances," Grandpa explained. "I remembered things I hadn't thought of in decades. Things about my own mother. Her smell. The feel of her hand holding mine."

"Where am I going?" the Grandpa on the floor said, and I heard the sadness ringing in his voice like the toll of a bell. "I am alone."

"Everything was dark," Grandpa whispered.

"We have to help him," I said.

"No," Grandpa said. "We can't. I don't know what will happen. We've come too far already."

On the floor, Grandpa groaned. And I felt the groan trigger a feeling deep in my own insides. I felt a tugging, as if something that belonged inside was being pulled out. I broke away from Grandpa to get to the man on the floor.

I picked his head up and laid it in my lap. It was surprisingly heavy. "I feel him!" I shouted.

Grandpa rushed over to my side. "I can't see," mumbled the man on the floor. I touched his hand. I curled my fingers around his palm, and even though he could no longer get his hand to move, I knew he felt mine.

"He can feel me!" I said.

"Oh, Michael," Grandpa cried. "This is not good. You don't *want* him to feel you."

I didn't care. I leaned down close to Grandpa's ear, where I thought he could hear me best. "It's me, Michael," I said.

At first, I didn't think he heard. But then, his cheek muscles twitched. "An angel?"

"Your grandson."

"Ahh." He was able to move his hand just a little now. It felt like he was trying to squeeze mine. "Where am I going?" he said. "I don't know where I'm going."

"Let go of that wretched man," Grandpa cried. "Oh, Michael! You have to let him be."

"But he's dying," I protested. "Can't you feel how this is better?"

"It's not better," he said.

I tried to remember what Grandpa had told me before, the first time he had taken me into the river of the dead. "Where you're going doesn't hurt," I told him. "And you don't just disappear. You'll see me, and you'll see Grandma—Stella. You'll see my dad."

"Ahh," he said. He opened his eyes and looked at me. His eyes were the same brown as Ghost Grandpa's but dimmer. His lids hung heavy like he was about to fall asleep. "Thank you," he said, though he was more mouthing the words than saying anything I could hear. Then he said, "I'm letting go," and closed his eyes back down.

That's when—I think—he died. I felt a shiver of cold, and I remembered later that I heard a sound like a door opening quietly and clicking closed.

But at the time, I was just staring at Grandpa's face. It was a different face from the ghost of Grandpa I'd gotten to know. It was thinner, somehow, older looking. It looked like he was sleeping, except he was too still for that.

I turned, to tell Grandpa that he really was gone. But Grandpa was no longer there.

Letting go of the dead man's hands, I stood. I tried not to panic. "Grandpa?" I called out. Where was he? "Grandpa?" I looked in the bathroom. I checked underneath the bed. I even climbed the ladder into the sleeping loft, which was filled with the dusty magazines Dad and I would drag down later. I took two steps to the front door but shivered even contemplating the black abyss out there.

That's when I remembered the sound of the door opening and closing. "No," I said aloud. "Oh, no." How could Grandpa have left me alone?

Just then the door opened again, seemingly on its own. Grandpa! I thought. Boy, was I going to yell at him. How could he have given me such a scare?

But it wasn't Grandpa. It was paramedics, two of them, running. As soon as they saw the body on the floor, they dropped their kits and knelt down by Grandpa's side. A tall paramedic with a handlebar mustache felt for a pulse in Grandpa's neck. The other one, who was blond, with freckles, laid his hands one on top of another on Grandpa's chest and started to pump. "No," the tall one said. "He's got a Do Not Resuscitate order on file. He doesn't want us to pull him back."

The tall one pushed a button on the radio that was clipped to his belt. "He's passed," he said into the radio, nodding at the blond guy, who was catching his breath. "And he's got a DNR. We're going to load him up and bring him into the hospital to get it certified."

"Hey," I said to them when they started unpacking a duffel bag of equipment. They didn't look up. I tried tapping one of them on the shoulder, then the other, but my finger felt nothing but air. The short blond one shivered. "It's cold in here," he said.

"Let's damp down the stove," said the tall one, closing the

vent on the fire, which had burned down to almost nothing anyway.

I went to the light switch and flicked the lights on and off.
"What was that?" said the blond.

"What was what?" said the tall one.

"You didn't see the lights just flicker?"

"Oh, you," he said. "You and your ghosts." The short guy
went red in the face. I concentrated really, really hard, and got
him to look at my reflection in the dark window, but he pretended he hadn't seen it. I remembered something Ewan had
said. Most people don't see ghosts, and the ones who do pretend
they don't, because they're scared.

But *was* I a ghost? To become a ghost, you need to die.

In a flurry of motion, the paramedics zippered Grandpa's
body into a bag and strapped him to a neon yellow stretcher.
They checked the cabin to make sure it was empty, turned out
the lights, and closed the door.

After they left, the silence was enormous. It wasn't the dark
that scared me as much as it was the sound of the wind in the
trees, and the rattling of something out on the porch. Most people alone in a dark cabin would be afraid of ghosts. No one ever
thinks how scary it is to *be* a ghost. Or to think you might be one.

Where was Grandpa? How could he leave me here all by
myself? I started to get really, really cold. I sat down on the bed
and pulled the blanket up to my chin. With a sense of sureness I
never felt before, I knew I was stuck. I was stuck, and I was alone.

Grandpa had said that when he'd been lying on the floor,

177

dying, the shell over his heart had cracked. I closed my eyes. Waiting for something that I knew very well wasn't going to come, something cracked around my heart as well.

I must have been lying there an hour, not moving, feeling tired the way you do when you have a high fever. I started to think about Grandpa's memories of the war, and soon I felt like I was inside them again, alone on the hillside with the burning pain in my knee. I saw myself playing basketball in the gym at Selden, winning. It didn't matter. Soon, I couldn't tell if I was me playing, or Grandpa watching me while he was in the war. I didn't know if I was going to make it off the hill. None of my balls were going into the basket. Grandpa had had to keep moving to stay alive in the war, to pull himself off the field and into the woods. And what had my dad said when we were packing up the cabin in the cold? Keep moving, it's the only way to stay warm.

So I stood. I walked one circle around the cabin. I walked it again, making laps, circling over and over until eventually I noticed the letter Grandpa had been writing to my dad. The paper still lay on the table, glowing in the moonlight that came through the window, though I knew that there was really no moon—just the black night of the river.

What was it Grandpa wanted to say? I stepped closer to the table and lifted the paper. I was hoping for a secret, something that would release me. A map. Or a key. A message that could give me a clue as to how to get out. Or a message like the one I'd sent Ewan from his father before I knew what I was talking about.

But the paper said "Dear Daniel," and nothing more.

All those years, this was all Grandpa could say? He sat down every day to try to unlock his heart, and every single day he failed?

I wondered how Grandpa had felt, sitting at the table. What did he want to say so badly he tried over and over again, and still he could not?

Thinking about the possibilities, I felt my right hand twitch. It was nearly frozen, but I thought I might be able to grip the pen. I sat down at the table, and picked it up in a shaky, clawlike grasp. I started to write. •

Chapter 15

I'd been writing at the table in the cabin for what felt like hours when I began to hear a noise. It was an uneven knocking. I laid the pen down on the table, and the noise stopped.

I lifted my pen to keep writing, and heard the knocking again. Maybe one of the ropes tying the tarp down over the pile of firewood had come loose and was blowing against the cabin wall? Mostly, I was trying to convince myself that it wasn't anything alive. I was afraid. If I opened the door again, what would happen to me? Was there some kind of monster of darkness that would suck me into the river?

Of course, I thought, the rapping might be Grandpa trying to get back in. The idea cheered me. If he were here, I wouldn't be lonely or scared. But still, I didn't know. Sometimes in video games, if you open a locked door, you walk right through. Other times, you fall off a cliff. Was the knocking just a test?

I stood. I waited. I listened. I waited some more, then took six steps across the room and put my hand on the knob. Again, I heard the noise. It was too solid to be anything but an intentional knock—someone was definitely out there. I started to twist the knob, then stopped. I prepared myself. I was hoping that if I opened the door, I'd find Grandpa. But, maybe, instead, the cabin walls would dissolve, leaving me alone in the river, without Grandpa to protect me, without a tunnel to lead me back into the world where I belonged. My heart was beating so quickly I felt I could hear the rushing of the blood through its valves. Finally, I closed my eyes and flung open the door.

There was nothing but the cold dark force pushing against me.

Then I heard a slapping sound and saw four fingers wrapped around the door frame. The fingers looked red from the cold and they were straining to hold on to the edge of the door. I jumped back. There was something familiar about the fingers.

I had an idea. I stood with my back against the wall next to the door and moved sideways toward the fingers. The force of the blackness was coming through the door, but when I came from the side, I was able to touch the ends of the red, freezing fingers with my own. As soon as I touched them, I felt the cold push of the river fade. The air began to feel warm and light, like it might inside a helium balloon. I felt myself beginning to lift off the ground. I smelled lemon pie—hot, sweet, and delicious. I looked down to check—I was definitely floating. I tried to put my feet on the floor, but I couldn't do it.

I began to float out the door, and I grasped the red, chapped hand even harder. I was feeling gentle and happy and full of light, but still, I knew there was danger. Whose hand was I holding? Where was I going?

As soon as I was out the door, I could see. The hand belonged to Gus. His body was plastered against the wall of the cabin, like he was inside one of those g-force spinning cylinder rides at an amusement park where people's hair sticks up, and some people can climb the wall, and eventually the floor drops out, and someone pukes and the puke goes flying onto the person next to them, and it is the grossest thing you've ever seen.

"Michael," Gus said. It was hard to understand him because the air was pushing his cheeks back toward his ears. It looked like he was baring his teeth. How come I wasn't feeling it? "Look!" he shouted, and gestured by moving his eyes away from me. The space inside the river was shaped very strangely—Gus's body looked like stretched-out Silly Putty. His other hand and even his face seemed very far away.

I followed his gaze to see who was holding his other hand. She looked as small as if she were standing on the other side of a football field, but I could still see who it was—Julia. She was floating out in the space beyond the porch, her toes pointed into a perfect second position, her eyes closed, her ponytail sticking straight up in the air as if she'd just stuck a knife into a toaster.

Beyond Julia, even smaller, was Trip. And beyond Trip was Ewan—a tiny Ewan. They were holding hands, making a chain. A chain of people. My friends. Against the impenetrable dark of the river, they looked like they were glowing yellow and pink.

"You guys are inside the river!" I shouted to Gus, half triumphant that they'd come to rescue me, half terrified that they were all stuck now in the same place I was.

"You have to come home now!" Gus shouted. "You have to hurry. Ewan said just to tell you to climb onto me."

"What are you even doing here? How did you get into the river?"

"Shut up, Michael," said Gus. "Start climbing."

But I was scared, and Gus did not look like he was safe. I knew what the cold felt like. I didn't want to go. "I'm not as strong as you guys," I said.

"Michael," Gus said, "don't you see? You have to try."

"It's warm where I am right now." I took a deep breath. "The air smells good all of a sudden. This is so comfortable. You go back. I'll stay here."

"You're not feeling *comfortable!*" Gus shouted. "You're feeling life. You're breathing in my life. And Julia's and Trip's and Ewan's. Ewan said to tell you how this is working. That you are stuck in the river right now and you don't have enough life force left to get out of it on your own. If you feel good right now, it's because you're sucking off the life force of all of us making this chain. Do you feel like the air is sweet? That's how your grandpa felt when he was with you."

"Oh my God," I said. He was right. Lemon. He'd said lemon pie.

"Michael, don't you see?" Gus went on. "You're drowning. You're dying. And if you don't come right away, you're going to take the rest of us with you."

"I told you, I can't!" I shouted, but I looked at him as I said it, and he looked back at me, hard, and held my gaze. I remembered sitting at the top of the jungle gym at the elementary school with him, jumping off farther than I thought I could go. I remembered running down the stairs of our building, pretending we were in a fire. I remembered the time we went to East Hampton with his dad and he let us ride to the Dairy Queen in the trunk of his Saab—it was so dark we couldn't see our own knees, and we held hands, like we were doing now.

And in that moment of feeling Gus's strength, I borrowed some of it, and I let go of his hand. A cold rush swept the warm floaty air away, but there was a split second when I had the chance to move. I kind of hurled myself at Gus's body, grabbing him. As the cold rushed in I felt its full impact and I knew I could no sooner have moved through it as I could have lifted a car. My body was being squeezed by the air around me.

"Climb across me," Gus said. "Climb right down the chain."

"I can't," I said again, but I started to move. Working my way across him was slow, and it reminded me of rock climbing. You find a place to put your hand, and then another place to put your foot. Each time I shifted, I felt like I was lifting a heavy stone. It took a lot of concentration, and it was exhausting. I didn't think I could make it to the end of Gus's body, much less down the rest of the chain.

I closed my eyes to rest, and without warning, I found myself inside Gus's mind, totally oblivious to what was happening with my body. It was a new kind of slipping. I saw Gus's mom, or at least her knees, from under a table. I was Gus, crawling and rolling on the floor under a table, with shoes everywhere. There were brown oxfords, and strappy, jeweled sandals, bare toes. The grown-ups were laughing loudly, and I could hear the clinking of forks on plates. I was remembering how I was laughing with them, almost like someone was tickling me. Colors inside this memory appeared brighter and the edges of things crisper and more tightly drawn. Happy! No wonder Gus is so good at everything he does.

Reinvigorated, I pulled myself all the way across Gus's body and was getting ready to cross over to Julia when I slipped inside Gus's mind again. This time, it didn't feel so happy. I was looking into a mirror and seeing an older Gus looking back at me. He had grown jowly around the jawline, and he had a full growth of beard, but his eyes were the same. Or rather, they were Gus's same black eyes, but they were sad. The bright light from earlier was gone. There were shadows in the mirror, and his eyelids were half lowered like he was trying not to fall asleep.

"What's wrong?" I said, without even thinking, and as I spoke, the vision changed. He caught his reflection in the mirror and I knew that part of what he was seeing there was me. And I wondered for the first time—I'd always thought that Gus had everything he needed, but maybe he needed me also?

And then I felt Julia's skinny-minny wrist between my ankles and I couldn't believe she would be strong enough to support me.

"Michael!" she shouted. I looked up at her face. She was crying, the tears traveling back toward her hairline like raindrops on the windshield of a moving car. "Michael, come on. You have to keep climbing."

"Are you okay?" I said, but she just shook her head.

I climbed along her body just as I had Gus's. The muscles in my arms and legs were starting to burn, and when I stopped, I found myself slipping into Julia's mind, just as I'd done with Gus. When Julia was little, she had a mirror in the car, in front of her seat, and she would talk to herself in it. I was her now, talking to the mirror, pretending I was a fancy lady who worked in a jewelry store, drawing my pretend long, painted fingernails across a pretend glass counter, saying, "Here are the diamonds. Here are the rubies." I opened my eyes ready to keep going, as energized by the idea of those imaginary diamonds and rubies as Julia had been as a kid.

It wasn't long before I was exhausted again, and again I slipped into her mind. This time, I was Julia standing at the back of Selden's auditorium. The seats were filled for assembly and I scanned through group after group, looking for a place to sit, a friend, or someone who might become a friend. Each empty seat was all wrong. And then Julia was inside the dance studio, a room where everything was either painted white or covered in mirrors, and she was spinning, her eyes fixed on her face in the mirror as she spun, and the light on the mirror was splitting into thousands of shards reflected off thousands of shiny, angled surfaces, and it hurt, but she had to keep making the pirouettes—there was a number she was counting, and her body was trained to follow her mind. I felt like something was going to crack, maybe one of my bones, and I wondered how Julia could keep spinning, could keep going with the light breaking apart inside her eyes.

And then I opened my eyes and looked up at the real Julia,

186

and I understood that there were things I knew about her that she did not. I slept thirty feet from Julia every single night. We shared a bathroom, for Pete's sake. And yet, I hadn't bothered to pay attention. Julia was just as freaked out finding a seat in assembly as I was. She was beautiful, but she wasn't perfect. She was a mess. She was like me.

I wanted to say something to her, the kind of thing you say if you're worried this may be the last thing you ever say. "You're the one who is beautiful," I said, and Julia nodded. I think she was doing everything she could to hold on and couldn't really take in what I was trying to say. I kept looking at her, though, and finally she nodded again, and I moved on.

Holding on to Trip I felt an instant rush of strength. With Gus, I'd felt the power of his happiness. With Julia, I'd felt energized by her quest for perfection. With Trip, I felt strong, traveling with the kind of athletic grace that belonged only to him.

But even so, climbing was hard work, and I had to rest. I slipped right inside his head, where I was standing in an open field, and there was a ball coming toward me. I caught it and threw it back to a man who looked like an older version of Trip. Was that Trip's dad? He was throwing the ball hard. "'Atta boy," he'd say when I caught it. "Get 'em," and "Yeah." With each catch, I heard myself grunting, but I never let a single ball drop.

And this is the surprising part: I was terrified of the ball. I was terrified of my dad. He was throwing the ball too hard on purpose. He wanted me to drop it.

"It's too hard!" I shouted. "I want to stop."

"No quitting," he said. "You want to be a man, right?" I didn't want to be a man. I wanted the balls to stop. So I threw them back so hard that my dad would be the one who couldn't catch them. But I couldn't win. The ball kept coming back at me.

I opened my eyes and was looking up at Trip's face. He'd made me feel powerful and strong right up until the moment when I'd slipped inside his head. Then I felt weak, angry, and scared. I didn't like being Trip.

I was afraid to close my eyes again, but I had to. This time, I saw something from Trip's future. Trip was saying, "Shh, it's okay." He—or I—was holding a woman's hand. I knew that I was calming her down, that I had the strength to control her feelings with my voice. Her hand was bloody. It was sticking out of the window of a car. The car was dented—no, it was crushed, and half flipped over, such that the side window was facing the sky, and I was holding the strange woman's hand as an ambulance siren sounded from far away. "You're going to be okay," I was saying. "Shh, now. I'm not going to leave you here." And I sounded like a girl, I was making my voice so high and soft. I asked the woman for her name. "Annie," I said, after she'd told me. "Annie, you should see the desert out here. It's like nothing else. When you get out of this car, I'm going to show you these purple mountains. You'll see what I mean."

While I was inside this memory, I didn't know where Trip was, or who this person in the car was, but I knew that the energy Trip was passing on to me as I climbed across him was also flowing into Annie. Trip was generous—I understood that now—and he was giving something from inside himself to a stranger.

And then my eyes were open and I started to slide down his arm, really fast, as if he were pushing me away.

"You go, dude," Trip said. He did have the power to make me feel calm, just like he'd done with the woman in the crashed car. "You're all good. Keep it up."

As soon as I latched on to Ewan, I immediately went into his mind, and I felt a shock so painful I nearly let go. What was happening inside Ewan wasn't a vision or a memory. It was right now. I was running along that gray curve of road that he draws over and over in art class, the same road I saw when I was sitting next to him in assembly. I was alone, under the low sky.

"Ewan," I said, forcing my eyes open and looking up at his stringy hair and long eyelashes. He was screwing up his face, and I could feel his arm muscles tightening. "Move along," he said. "I can't stand this."

And then something happened on the road. I ran to the edge, looked over, and saw the red car. It was turned upside down at the bottom of a gully—it must have just crashed, because there was smoke coming from the smashed-up engine, and I heard a hissing sound of steam.

Was this the same car that Trip had found? Did Trip rush down the side of the mountain and hold someone's hand inside the car? Trip had said it was the desert, and this was not a desert. It was not the same car. But I remembered what Grandpa said about what memories he traveled to in the river—there were connections between them.

The car I was seeing in Ewan's head was much more badly

189

smashed than the one in Trip's. I knew no one could have sur-
vived. And yet, while I looked down from above, a man in a red
jacket was standing next to it. He looked familiar to me, but I
couldn't place him. When he saw me, he started to run up the
cliff, scrambling on the rocks, and I scrambled down, and then we
were standing together, and the man was holding me, and I was
sobbing, and I was saying, "Is this real?" and he was saying, "It's as
real as it needs to be," and I was saying, "Why are we here?" and
he said, "To say good-bye."

But then he was sobbing too, and I was the one holding him,
and he was saying, "I'm not ready to go."

"I'm not ready to have you go," I said.

"Ewan!" I shouted, opening my eyes, forcing myself out of his
head, or at least trying to. "Keep going, Michael," he said. "It's
time to go."

"Are you sure?" I said.

"Just go!" he shouted. And I knew how strong he had to be
to tell me to move, because by now I'd recognized the man in
the red jacket from Ewan's earth science report. He was Ewan's
dad, and Ewan was telling me to push past him. He was saying
good-bye.

And so I closed my eyes and squeezed Ewan as hard as I
could, a big bear hug like the one Grandpa had meant to give me
when we were swimming in the water. *Good-bye*, I thought. And
inside Ewan's mind I saw his dad feeling the strength of my hug to
Ewan. I saw both of them taking deep breaths, and then his dad
let go. "You go on," he said. "Do not stay here with me." And

then Ewan said to him, "You are inside me. You are the best parts of me," and his dad said, "I'll be watching over you," and I released my hug. I was hardly able to breathe through my sobs. I felt like Ewan was my best friend, like he was precious to me, like it was going to be my job now to take care of him and make sure he was okay.

"Michael," he muttered, and I knew how much strength he must be using to speak. "Go," he said. "Go on." And so I did.

As I traveled down Ewan's arm, I tried to lift my head to see who was waiting for me on Ewan's other side, but a current of air knocked it back down. I didn't see until I was actually crossing over. It was my dad.

As soon as I touched his wrist, I knew I would be okay. I understood, just for a second, how much my dad loves me. He loves me as much as Ewan and his dad loved each other. He loves me with the strength of Trip's grace. His love has the power of Julia's beauty. He loves me with all of Gus's brilliance, and his hope.

For one second, in the first moment of touching him, I felt like I had when I was little and my dad was holding me and I was resting my head on his shoulder. I had never made this connection before, but it was the same feeling I had had sitting on Grandpa's lap in the cabin, when we were watching him die, when he was whispering the list of everyone he loved, and I'd felt there was no difference between the hot breath coming from his body and the breath I held inside my own.

But as I moved across my father, I felt the force of his energy rushing me. The feeling was like my body was being stretched. My stomach clenched with the effort, and I felt my jaw tightening. I couldn't see any memories—my dad was not letting me in. But I had to rest, so I closed my eyes and must have gone back into my own mind. I was seeing my memories of Grandpa. Grandpa writing at his lonely table in the cabin. Grandpa watching Grandma at their school when Grandpa wasn't brave enough to say hello or even smile. Grandpa on that open field before the battle, closing his mind to thoughts that could make him go soft.

Dad tried to pull me past these memories, but I pulled the other way. It felt almost as if Grandpa was the one pulling back while my dad pushed me forward. I felt tiny against their force. We were all three of us locked together.

"Michael," my dad said.

"Grandpa," I said back.

But as I held on to my dad, his pulling turned into a pulse. A giant, throbbing pulse that was highly invigorating. It gave me the energy to keep going. There was absolutely no way to see inside him, past the pulsing light of his demands. But at least I knew now what his number one demand was, and it was really simple. He wanted me to live. The pulse inside him wasn't in his mind. It was in his chest. It was his heart. It was sending out a signal that was jump-starting mine. With each wave of electric reaction, I felt a cascade of sparks inside my body.

"Michael, hold on," my father was muttering over and over. "Two seconds more. Hold on. Hold on." I remembered what Grandpa had said in the cabin. "I love you more than I love my life." And I felt that in my father's strength, even as I felt his grip weakening and my legs beginning to float behind me into the cold, rushing void.

Then, with no warning, I landed hard on the wooden cabin floor. I could see my own body—I was next to it. I was lying on the floor, and sitting around me in a circle were my dad, Ewan, Gus, Trip, and Julia. They all had their eyes closed.

"I'm here!" I called, but they didn't move. "I'm back!" Had they heard? Without knowing how, I knew what to do, I felt myself drawn toward my own body, looking down into it, seeing that it was really me. For the last time, I had the feeling of slipping. Except this time, instead of slipping into the cold river of the dead, I was slipping into the warmest, safest bed that I'd ever known.

"Wake up," I said into the circle as soon as I was in my body once more. No one moved. Ewan was squeezing his eyes shut, trembling, his freckles dark against his pale skin. Gus's face was set in perfect stillness, the utterly blank look he sometimes gets when he is playing sports. Trip was sneering. Julia's face was contorted in her perfect fake smile. Dad's head was bowed, and he looked a way I had never seen him before. I can only describe it as wasted. His cheeks were hollowed, his hair starting to curl. Had he lost weight? I couldn't believe a person could change like that in just a few—hours? Minutes? How long had I been gone?

Ewan was the first to open his eyes. He closed them again as if he hadn't even seen me, and gave a shake to his hands, which sent a ripple through everyone else in the group. One at a time they opened their eyes and dropped hands.

"Michael," Dad said, looking at me to see that I was awake. "Oh, Michael. Thank God."

Trip raised a fist in a gesture of triumph. "Yeah!" he shouted, and looked around the room, desperate for someone to high-five.

Julia's eyes popped open like someone had pushed her from behind. Tears started to stream down Ewan's pinched little face.

Gus opened his eyes just a crack, then collapsed forward onto his forearms, his face touching the floor. "Get him a blanket," Ewan said, though he looked like he himself might go into shock, and Julia took off her coat and passed it over, though her teeth were chattering too.

"What happened?" I said, but they were all just staring at me, as if they couldn't believe I was there.

Chapter 16

After we recovered, my dad lit a fire in the woodstove and turned the gas on so we could boil water. He found mugs in one of the boxes of dishes he'd left for Goodwill, and he made us all drink a cup of hot tea—he'd found tea bags too. "I guess it's good I'm so cheap I saved this," he said about the tea, and it was weird to hear him admit to something like that.

While we drank our tea, my dad kept asking all of us questions like, "What's the date today?" and "Who is president?" and except for the fact that Gus had no idea what the date was—he never does—we all gave answers that satisfied my dad we didn't have concussions, or whatever he was worried about.

All of us were pretty exhausted. Or at least I know I was. I wanted to go to sleep, but I was still too cold, even with my parka zipped up to my chin, and the blankets my dad found in a box by the door wrapped around my legs. I had a lot of questions, but I didn't know where to start and it was hard to get a word in edgewise with my dad asking everyone how many fingers he was holding up, and running around fetching things to make us feel better. Julia, Trip, Ewan, and Gus were staring into space a lot, like they were doing math problems in their heads. But my dad seemed full of effi-ciency. I would have said he seemed happy, if he also didn't seem kind of zombielike. His eyes weren't connecting with anyone's, and sometimes he sort of slurred his words, he was talking so fast.

Finally, he said, "Come on. We can't spend the night here. We have to go home," and without waiting for an answer, he went outside to shovel out the car.

There was a minute of total silence when he was gone, and then I looked up from the floorboard I was staring at—it had a knot that looked a little bit like a silhouette of a rabbit—and said, "How did you guys even get up here?"

I think they were all too exhausted to answer, and so they each waited for someone else to speak up. When no one did, Julia said, "I drove." Speaking seemed to wake her up a bit, and she went on. "I thought you were sleeping, and I went to get you around nine. When I saw you weren't there, I kind of freaked out. Mom told me what had happened. I texted Gus, who got everyone else together, and then I told Mom I was going to get something to eat in the kitchen, then snuck out of the service entrance and ran to the garage and got the car."

"But you don't have a license," I said.

"No," she said. "But it seemed like it might be an emergency. And it was."

"We got here just after you'd slipped," Ewan continued. "Your dad must have been with you, because when he saw our car pulling up to the house he ran out screaming for help. He didn't know it was us."

"I kind of panicked when I saw him and drove the car into a ditch," Julia explained.

"Which really made your dad go ballistic," said Trip. "Because he couldn't get his car out of the snow either, and so there was no way anyone could go for help."

"Did you explain to him?" I started. I could hardly figure out how to ask the question, it was so hard to imagine a scenario in which my dad would even listen to the story of what had been happening to me. "Did he understand?"

"I tried," Ewan said. "But he didn't believe me."

"You did awesome," Trip said to him. "Ewan made us all sit in a circle and hold hands, and he started to chant."

"Your dad was furious," Gus said. "But there wasn't anything he could do. He kept slapping his cell phone against the wall. Then he would stand over you, shouting, 'Michael, wake up, I'm serious, you have to wake up.'"

"But after a while," said Trip, "it wasn't like before, when you were shaking and stuff? You were hardly breathing."

"I'd read about this technique for reaching people who have just died," Ewan said. "You can go in after them by making a chain with people who know the person and who want to reach them."

"How did you convince my dad to help?"

"We didn't," Ewan said. "We started the chain without him. After we had all gone into the trance, we couldn't see what was happening here in the cabin. But it was good he joined on."

"How did the chain work?"

"It was crazy," said Gus. "It kind of reminds me of what you said it was like to slip. Or at least what it was like to be inside the river. Everyone held hands, except Ewan and I were each holding one of your hands. And then we started chanting this word Ewan told us to chant—"

"It's something Charlisse told me, just as we were leaving her house," Ewan jumped in. "She said it really casually, as if it might be something I was mildly curious about. She said, when building river chains, chanting helps, and she likes to pick as her chant the word 'fluvius,' which is Latin for river. It doesn't matter whether you chant or not, it's just a way to focus your concentration. The most important thing is that you're holding the person's hand, and that you are focused on getting him back." Ewan sounded a little bit like he was giving an oral report. It would have been annoying except I think I was done being annoyed with Ewan. It wasn't that he had saved me. It's that once you've seen all the way inside someone, you see them as they see themselves.

"Fluvius, fluvius," Gus said, and he shivered. "As we said it, I started to feel cold, and then kind of creepy, and then there was a pressure building on me, and then I wasn't holding your hand anymore, I was smashed up against the wall of the cabin, trying to reach you. I knew you were inside, and I had to bang my hand against the wall, like, a million times before you opened the door."

"How did you even know where to go?" I said. "How did you get to me?"

198

"We were holding on to your body. It was still connected to your soul."

"And did you know that Grandpa had left me alone?"

"No," Ewan said. "But I suspected it."

"We had come to the point in time where he died, and I watched him die," I started to explain, but I couldn't keep talking because I felt a lump forming in my throat.

"Are you okay?" Ewan said, and I took a deep breath.

I explained how alone Grandpa had felt, how he was scared, and how I held his head and talked to him. "When I looked up," I finished, "the Grandpa who had been with me all along was gone."

"You gave him what he wanted," Ewan said, as if I'd finally solved the riddle.

"But I still don't really know what that was."

"Don't you see?" Julia said. I might have found her question show-offy before, but as with Ewan, I saw her differently now. She was trying to help me. "You gave him love. You showed him that someone did love him."

"That must have made it possible for his spirit to dematerialize," Ewan continued. "He was able to die in peace. His soul was able to dissolve into the river instead of traveling through it, fighting against it all the while."

"Is that what happened with your dad?"

Ewan blushed, something I'd never seen him do, and suddenly the oral report tone of voice was gone. "I don't know," he mumbled. "I think my dad might still be out there."

"What are you talking about?" Trip asked.

"Nothing," I said, because I didn't want to make Ewan have to explain it to everybody.

But Trip already knew. "Are you talking about saying goodbye to your dad?" he asked. Ewan nodded. "That was amazing," Trip went on. "I'm so sorry, man."

"It's not a big deal," Ewan muttered.

"I remember seeing Ewan with his dad too," Gus said. "When was that?"

"It was in the chain," I said.

"I saw it," said Julia. "It's like I can hardly remember it, though. It's like it was a dream."

"I guess everyone was seeing what I saw with everyone else," I said. "I thought it was just me."

"You saw me in the car, right?" said Julia. And then her face kind of blanched. "And at assembly."

Gus looked a little stricken too. I wondered if he was thinking about how his older face in the mirror had looked so sad.

"Oh, God," said Trip, and I wondered what bothered him more, seeing himself in the future, or being afraid of the ball.

"I can't believe I'm back here," I said. "I can't believe I'm actually alive." It's kind of like the first few days of summer vacation, when every few minutes you forget it's not just a weekend, and you remember, and it totally makes you happy every time. "I'm just so glad to be back."

"But Michael," Ewan said, "are you ready for it to be over?"

And that's the thing. Happy as I was to feel safe again, I

wasn't done. I was scared and exhausted, but I had questions. I missed Grandpa.

"In the end," I said, "I was all alone. Grandpa left me alone. To die. How could he have done that?"

"He probably didn't know," said Ewan. "Most of what was happening to you was out of his control. His energy came from his loneliness and his fear, which were released into the world when he was dying. But as soon as you changed the way he died, you dissolved that energy. He probably didn't want to leave you. But you made him so warm and comfortable, he was able to just slip away."

"I heard the door close," I said.

"But maybe it wasn't the cabin door," Ewan suggested. "Maybe it was a door inside your mind. Maybe it was as much the door to the river that your grandfather walked through as it was a door that you passed through yourself."

"Wow," I said.

"You're stronger now," Ewan went on. "Your grandfather left a lot of himself behind in you."

"Wow," I said again. "But where did he go? Did he definitely dissolve? Or is there another place?"

"I don't know," Ewan said.

"Is there any way to find out?"

"Charlisse said you just have to think about it hard enough until you feel you know the truth."

"So he might come back? There's a chance?"

"Michael," Ewan said, "it's important that you let him go. You have to let him rest."

"Okay," I said, but it wasn't okay. I wanted Grandpa back.

"You know," said Gus, "it was really your dad who saved you. When you started to climb, that must have been when your dad grabbed on to Ewan's hand. I felt a change. I didn't think I could hold on another second, banging on that door, and then suddenly, I felt the whole chain grow stronger."

"Really?" I said. "He was definitely the strongest one of all of you when I was climbing. It was kind of painful how much he was pushing me along."

Trip looked out the window and said, "He doesn't look so strong now," and when we all joined him, we saw that my dad was trying to shovel, but every time he set the shovel into the snow, he kind of collapsed over it, and he could hardly lift it out when it was loaded.

"We should help him," said Julia, and everyone started to stand.

"Not you," said Ewan, to me. "You need to rest."

And that's how, after they sent my dad inside to drink a cup of tea, I ended up alone with him in the cabin.

He was sitting on the edge of Grandpa's bed, wrapped in Grandpa's quilt.

"What made you join the chain?" I asked him. He looked too exhausted to speak, but I couldn't look at him another second, or say anything else to him, before I knew the answer to that question.

"I didn't mean to," he said. "I was just scared, Michael. I was watching you die, and there was nothing I could do. So I took your hand from your friend Ewan and I held it and I said your name over and over again, and I called for you to come back, and you did."

"Dad, I was with Grandpa," I said, not because I thought he was going to believe me, but because I needed him to know. "I saw him die. I made it okay for him."

"Michael," he said, "Ewan said some of that to me already, and I don't know what to believe."

"Grandpa did love you," I said. "I mean, he does."

"That's just great," he said bitterly. "It's too bad he had such a poor way of showing it."

"He tried," I started to say, and just as I was thinking that there was no way I could make him believe me, I remembered something. "Here," I said, opening the drawer to the table. The letter I had written was there, folded into triangles like notes girls pass in school. My father's name was written on the outside. The handwriting was Grandpa's, not mine. "This is for you."

"For me?" said my dad. It took him a few minutes to untangle the complicated folding job. His hands were unsteady. Brow furrowed, he ran the bottom of his fist over the creases in the page, which is something he does when he reads magazines, as if he'll be so bothered by the folds in the page he won't be able to read the words.

Once the paper lay flat, he read the letter through all the way, then started reading it again. I saw him grimace, and then turn red, and then cover his nose with his fist as if he was holding back a sneeze. After a long time, he crumpled the letter into a ball, shoved it deep inside his pocket, sat on the bed, and covered his face with his hands.

Here is what the letter said:

Dear Daniel,

I want you to know that I was once a boy. A boy who polished red shoes and tugged at his mother's legs while she worried over pennies. I was a boy who laughed at the movies, who cried over broken toys, who learned to walk quietly in apartments crowded with relatives.

For me, becoming a man was a lesson in protection. I protected myself from feelings of all kinds—fear, mostly, but in the end, also love. I know now that it's impossible to protect yourself from some feelings without protecting yourself from them all. I am sorry for the love that I took from you, but I am more sorry for the lessons you learned from watching me.

I want to protect you still—from my pride, my love, my envy, as it will awake in you feelings of loss and pain. But I know now that to protect you is to steal from you your right. This is my last will. This is what I leave to you. That I am your father. That you are my son. That every day since you were born I have loved you. That I love you now, in silence and from a great distance away.

Respectfully,
Your father

I wanted to explain to Dad how Grandpa tried to write the letter every day but hadn't been able to. I wanted to explain to him that when I wrote it, I hadn't been me, that I had been Grandpa. In my memory, I heard the scratching on the paper over the wind, and yet I don't remember writing those words.

I ended up not saying anything at all.

. . .

After the others came in from shoveling out the Jeep, Dad left his Mercedes behind and drove us down to New York, where my mom met us in the lobby. She is the kind of person who can sense when it's better not to ask a lot of questions, and she didn't say anything about Julia's skipping a *Sleeping Beauty* rehearsal, or taking her car. What she did say was one word, "Soup." After a shower, we changed into our pajamas, and Julia and I watched her put carrots, celery, and bouillon cubes into a pot. I had no idea she knew how to do that. My dad locked himself in the bedroom. He didn't come out until the next morning when he went to work, even though it was Sunday.

I haven't seen much of him since. I think the letter from Grandpa—and the things he saw inside me when we were in the river of the dead—they might have backfired. It's like now that Grandpa admitted to him that he wasn't a very good dad, it's possible for my dad to admit the same thing—but not to do anything about it. The letter didn't make him want to be closer to me—or even Julia. I think it just freaked him out. Julia says she thinks it embarrassed him.

He isn't rushing me off to school, screaming and yelling the whole time. He isn't telling me to stop playing video games. He isn't going through the stuff in my room. He isn't making plans and canceling them. He isn't even showing up for let's-pretend-we-do-this-every-night family dinners.

Mom isn't happy with the mystery, or the silence. One night when I was playing *NBA Street* and she was checking e-mail on her laptop next to me, my dad came in from work and walked straight into the kitchen, grunting instead of saying hi. Mom waited a few minutes, then opened the swinging door that connects the dining room to the kitchen and watched him at the blender. "Daniel?" she said, but I don't think he heard. She went back to the computer, but she didn't type anything more.

On one of the rare Sundays he was around at breakfast time, my mom said she wanted to call a travel agent about a spring break trip to the Bahamas, and my dad shrugged. "You know we never go on the trips we plan," he said. They were talking in the kitchen while Julia and I were watching TV, but we heard them. "Why do we go through this charade?"

"Julia and Michael will be disappointed," my mom said.

"They're already disappointed," said my dad. "So what's the point of pretending?" I wanted to run into the room and tell him it wasn't true, but at the same time, it kind of was.

Chapter 17

The last day of school before March vacation was shockingly warm. Kids peeled off their neckties, rolled up their sleeves, and we didn't even bother carrying our balled-up tweed blazers from one class to another. By lunchtime the lacrosse guys were walking around in shorts.

"Please let us have class in the park," whined annoying Tori Lublin in history, in art, in ethics. "We'll concentrate," she said. "We promise we will." But in the fall, one of Selden's seniors had eaten a vendor hot dog in the park during an outdoor English seminar, got food poisoning, and missed her interview at Princeton. None of the teachers budged.

It was the last day before the break, so there were no sports, and we were free to go when the bell rang at the end of eighth period. Usually, on the day before vacation, my mom makes us rush right home from school to help her pack. My mom hates packing, and the suitcases are always still open at ten o'clock when my dad comes home with the bad news that he can't go away, by which point we're all kind of relieved, since it's better to know for sure than to be guessing—guessing is why we hadn't been able to pack in the first place. But Julia and I hadn't heard any updates about travel plans. As far as we knew, we weren't traveling at all.

Gus found Ewan and me at my locker. Gus's parka was stuffed into the straps of his book bag, and he was holding a soccer ball under his arm. He was wearing a Hawaiian shirt under his oxford in honor of the fact that he was flying to Hawaii with his dad, Buffy, and his stepsisters the next day.

"Want to kick the ball around in the park?" he said.

Ewan shot me a look, like he was checking to see if Gus meant both of us or just me. Ewan was carrying an extra-heavy duffel bag, full of books he was planning to bring home and read over the break.

Gus hadn't seen Ewan's look, but he said, "Yeah, you too, Greer. Bring your inhaler."

Since Vermont, Julia's, Trip's, Gus's, Ewan's, and my thoughts had been connected. We slipped in and out of one another's minds, feeling when we were there the traces of one another's steps. When Julia emerged from the tutu-wearing corps in *Sleeping Beauty*, I'd felt sick to my stomach with her fear. I'd felt her pride when she took her bows, and had to hide my tears by booting up the Game Boy before the applause had died down. But Julia had known how I felt, just as Ewan knew when Trip hit a home run in baseball, and Ewan knew when any of us were stuck for an answer on a test (unfortunately, it wasn't the kind of connection where he could feed us the answers). It wasn't that we had psychic powers. Ewan made us all go back to Charlisse's dining room, but she just clapped her hands emphatically and said, "You're children, not mystics." It was more that we'd found a way to all be friends.

We walked down Fifth Avenue, Gus's ski jacket strapped to his back like he was carrying a giant pillow, mine flapping open. Ewan pushed his off his shoulders, trying to let in some air.

"Hey, wait up!" we heard, and saw Trip coming down Ninety-first Street. He was eating a slice of pizza folded in half inside a paper plate. For spring break, Trip was spending a week at his brother's college in Colorado. His brother went to the kind of college where your dorm room sits on a ski slope and there were boot dryers in the lounges.

"Did you finish the essay on the history final?" Trip asked Ewan when he'd caught up. In addition to eighth-grade history, Ewan was also taking the tenth-grade class with Trip. "I screwed up the multiple choice so bad that when I got to the essay, I was like, 'Oh, well.' And then the bell rang."

"I hated that stupid test," Ewan said. "He tried to fool us with that obvious citation from the Treaty of Versailles. If you're going to be tricky, fine, but he was just wasting our time, don't you think?"

"Yeah," said Trip, his voice emptying. "I guess I missed that one."

After we got back from Vermont, Trip had asked his mom— who served on Selden's board of trustees—to get Ewan out of work study for the spring so that he could play on the tennis team. It turned out Ewan was really good at tennis, as long as he used the inhaler. And now Ewan was helping Trip keep up a B average so that he could play baseball.

When we got to the park entrance just above the Met, Gus let the ball roll down his legs and started dribbling up a hill. We were next to a playground, where little kids were running from swings to sandbox, their hair sweaty, their nannies making them keep their winter coats on even though it was warm. Gus kicked the ball against the high iron playground fence, and it bounced to the other side of the path. My backpack banging against my body, I ran into the woods after the ball, kicking it ahead of Gus so he had to run too. Trip cut him off, lifting the ball on his toe and catching it in his hands.

"Ewan, think fast," he said, and threw the ball right at Ewan's chest. Ewan caught it, a little shakily, then kicked it over to me. Trip was always doing things like that to Ewan, but Ewan was starting to get used to it.

The four of us kicked the ball back and forth, jogging around the reservoir and down the bridle path. Just below Ninetieth Street, we cut over to the Great Lawn, which is a huge open area where you can play softball or just lie on the grass. Today it was surrounded by a temporary plastic fence, but Gus pushed a section of the fence down and we crossed over. The lawn was immense and glowing, like a lake, while the woods that we had passed through were already dark.

Ever since Gus and I got knocked off our bikes by kids from a different school when we were in fifth grade, I'd been afraid of coming to the park after dark. But now I'm not afraid of things the way I used to be. Maybe it's because I've started to grow. My mom took me to Dr. Horowitz just to make sure there wasn't anything wrong with me after I grew an inch in a month and had shooting pains in the bones of my ankles. "What exactly are you worried about?" Dr. Horowitz said. "Would you be happier if he were shrinking?" I can now stand up straight and carry the cello case on the stairs at school. When the upperclassmen pass me on the way to the lounge and laugh, I look them straight in the eye. But I don't really think I've stopped being afraid because I'm taller. I guess after Vermont, it's going to be a while before I'm afraid of anything again in ordinary ways.

When we reached the middle of the Great Lawn, Gus threw down his bag and jacket, picked up the soccer ball, and ran halfway across the field shouting in a fake English accent, "Keeper Edwardson with an amazing save! And he's running. He's running down the field. Wait! This is incredible! Do I believe my eyes? He's got Euro football confused with American, and no one's touching him."

"*Criiiiikey,*" Trip chirped. "One of the Italian defenders spots him! And he's chasing after him with amazing speed. It looks like he's going to use the full body tackle!"

I stood where I was, letting my bag slide down to the grass as well. I didn't know if I should run like Gus and Trip. I decided to run, but not toward the ball. I ran away from it, feeling the sponginess of the ground that was stiff from being still half frozen. As I gained speed, I lost the sensation that Trip and Gus were watching me. I ran and ran, and felt like I could go forever without ever reaching the other side of the plastic fence, without ever coming upon another path, another person, a tree.

Eventually, I circled back toward Trip and Gus. Gus saw me coming, and with Trip closing in on him, he threw the ball down onto the grass and kicked up a chip shot. I jumped harder and higher than I thought I could and felt a stinging in my palms as I pulled the ball to my chest. The ball felt like it was electrified.

Trip tackled me, hitting hard so that we both fell back onto the grass. "You dork!" I shouted, but I knew that it wasn't me he'd tackled, it was the ball. He would always—as long as he lived—go for the ball. I rolled on top of it now, and tried to keep it underneath me. Gus had taught me that if you want to break someone's grip you should go limp for a second before pulling away.

Finally I rolled clear of Trip, struggled to stand, and threw the ball up in the air as hard as I could, thinking that it was the only way to protect the ball and keep it safe. Gus, Trip, and I stopped, watching it twist into the dark and almost disappear before it reversed. Ewan was watching too. Time seemed to stop while the ball hung in the air, and with the four of us together, in the dark, I had a tiny electric memory of climbing across their bodies in the great dark they had saved me from.

When Gus caught the ball, he called out, "Spud!" I laughed and so did Trip, who was leaning over to catch his breath, his hands resting on his knees. I looked over my shoulder at Ewan to see if he got the joke, and that's when I saw the figure at the edge of the lawn.

It was a smudge against the woods, and I shuddered. I looked to either side. There was no one else around.

By now, all four of us were looking over at the figure—they'd seen him without my having to say a word. It wasn't that Gus, Trip, and Ewan were reading my mind. It was just that something made them look up and see the figure watching us from the other side of the fence. They knew without my having to say anything that I was worried. And maybe, without really knowing that they knew, they understood that we should all be worried because this man looked exactly like Grandpa.

He was too far away for me to really see him, but there were signs. The angle of his shoulders. The way he lifted his feet like he was being careful not to make any noise. The way he raised his arm over his head in a very particular wave.

I hadn't stopped missing him since we'd left Vermont. I hadn't lost the feeling I'd had in the cabin, waiting for him to come back, wondering how he could have left me when he'd told me that he loved me as much as his life. But now, with him watching us from beyond the fence, my feet grew heavy and my fingers cold. I was afraid—not of Grandpa, but of the cold. I was afraid of the emptiness I'd felt in the cabin when I was alone.

And then the figure stepped out from the woods and into the last little light that was coming from the sky, and I saw that it wasn't Grandpa. It was Dad.

I had never thought they looked alike, but now, I saw it. If my dad stooped a little, and cut his hair closer to his scalp, and if he got a tiny bit shorter, but stayed just as lean, my dad and Grandpa were the same.

My father stepped down over the plastic fencing and started

walking toward us on the field. Gus, who was still holding the ball, tossed it to me, and I caught it, easily. I could feel his relief— but I could also feel how Gus hadn't been worried. I don't know if I knew this from feeling it, or if I just knew Gus well enough to guess, but he'd been waiting to start worrying until the situation was clear. Trip was more curious than anything else, and Ewan had been busy analyzing the implications. Now I could feel them relax, but it was only in the vaguest way—sort of like someone's got a jackhammer going outside and you don't really notice it until it stops.

"What are you doing here?" I said to my dad, when he was close enough to hear me. I think I felt a little hopeful, a little excited, though I knew better by now. It's amazing how the door stays open. "Aren't you supposed to be at work?"

"Yes," said my dad. "I guess I should be. But I couldn't concentrate today. And I think the ice is cracking up on Grandpa's lake."

"Yeah?" I said. I tried not to sound too interested.

"Your mom tells me this is spring break week. I was thinking maybe we could get up there for the weekend and start working on clearing out some of the woods."

"Why?" I said, but I knew why. I hadn't thought of it, but it was exactly the right thing, to cut down trees Grandpa had let grow up between his porch and the sight of open water.

"We need to bury Grandpa," Dad went on. "All of us. Julia and you—your mother—we should all be there. To say goodbye."

I didn't say anything, because I couldn't. I might have cried. But also, I didn't want to interrupt my dad. I wanted him to keep talking, to finish saying what was in his head. "And for another thing," he went on, "I want a contractor to come in and look at the cabin. Maybe we can spend time there this summer. Or on weekends. You can bring your friends. I swam in that lake every summer when I was your age. Maybe it will feel a little warmer to you now that you're older."

"Okay," I said. I didn't want to sound like I cared too much. I still didn't know if this plan was just talk, or something that was really going to happen. But I liked the plan. A lot. I wanted to swim in the lake. I wanted my dad to teach me that dive he'd learned. And I wanted to bury Grandpa. I wanted to stand next to my dad and dig a hole in the ground at the top of the mountain where I knew Grandpa once stood looking at the view, eating a piece of salami. I wanted to tell my dad about that hike, and I wondered, was my dad going to listen?

He took a step closer, and he held up his hand. I threw a quick push pass, the kind I had made on the day Grandpa taught my body how to play basketball. My dad caught the ball and looked at me. I looked right back. I'd found Grandpa in his eyes before, and in my eyes Grandpa had found a way in. But right now, the only person I was seeing was my dad, and he was seeing me too. He spun the ball a few times in his hands, and then, still looking, he pushed it back to me, as if we were starting a game and he was checking in.

Acknowledgments

I wrote this book primarily at the New York Public Library and Au Bon Pain, and I am grateful for the use of their electricity and the banana nut muffins. I am more grateful to Rick Kahn; Sophie Bell; Claudia Gwardyak; Maribeth Batcha; Anita Kapadia; Arlaina Tibensky; Karen Shepard; Cassandra, Eve, and Ripley Cleghorn; Madeline McIntosh; Margaret Gray; Sarah Lynch; Debby Appelbaum; and Ed Mitre for reading this book while I was working on it and offering wisdom and advice. I am especially indebted to Lorri and Jordan Diggory and their mother-son book club—Logan and Alisa Kokx, and Avery and Shari Gnolek. I was blown away by their insights and inspired to keep going.

George Nicholson and Emily Hazel's enthusiasm and knowledge came like a bolt from the blue. Melanie Cecka's and Liz Schonhorst's tact, intelligence, and great warmth made the manuscript confident and strong.

My extended Bell-Kahn-Entin-Diggory-Breitbart-Gwardyak-Ouk family supports and inspires me. My father told me lots of great stories, my mother taught me from a young age that I was worth listening to, my sister laughs at my jokes, my children fill me with an important kind of joy, and, most especially, my husband, Rick, has always believed that this would happen.